For Virginia Raymon[...]

[...]u can plainly see my [...]vorite girl's name! Be [...]g[...]d — Cause you have i[...]

Amber Dean

READERS of *Dead Man's Float* and *Call Me Pandora* will want to follow this latest adventure of Abbie Harris, written with all of Amber Dean's freshness and unforced humor.

Abbie realizes she has a job on her hands when her nephew, Bill Hunt, comes to spend the summer and recuperate from a long and hard Pacific-theater service. Abbie had been warned by Bill's father that the boy was in a highly nervous state and should be watched carefully for signs of sudden anger. When Bill's army friend, who was also staying with them, is shot to death in a room which shows evidence of an almost psychopathic rage, Abbie is truly sick at heart, especially when Bill is unable to account for his actions during the time the killing took place.

Max Johnson, the detective who has helped Abbie before, again lends a hand, but reluctantly and only when impressed by Abbie's obvious distress.

When another murder takes place, apparently with no connection, Max refuses to believe that coincidence would stretch far enough to cause two violent deaths in a small community within forty-eight hours of each other, and it is from the clues of this second murder that he adroitly solves both killings.

This novel has not been serialized in any form prior to book publication.

WRAP IT UP

BOOKS BY AMBER DEAN

WRAP IT UP

 ## BY AMBER DEAN

**PUBLISHED FOR THE CRIME CLUB   1946
BY DOUBLEDAY & COMPANY, INC., GARDEN CITY, N. Y.**

179044

The idea for this story was given me by
Sherman Skuse.

Mommie and Max and their four little girls
are very real people. All other characters in
this book are fictitious.

WRAP IT UP

Bill walked through the house and found us on the front porch overlooking the lake. We didn't know him. Big and bony and blond, he had thinned down so in the four years since we had last seen him that his brown eyes, with their thick, girlish lashes, seemed to have sunken in under his straight, uncompromising brows.

He stood in the doorway to the living room and leaned a little against the frame. The look with which he brushed us moved swiftly to take in all of the immediate foreground. The crescent cove, the shallow water divided into pie-shaped pieces by the five docks leading from shore to deeper waters; the diving float, empty now.

I felt the fine hairs on my arms lift; a moment before I had been uncomfortably hot. A quick, surreptitious glance in Maggie's direction told me that a four-year-old memory was stirring, icily, uncomfortably, for her too.

He said, "Hello, Aunts."

Then I recognized him; I never forget a voice. I jumped up from the glider, threw my arms around him, and kissed him on a flat cheek. He hugged me and returned the kiss.

Maggie, who lacks my trigger reflexes, got up more slowly. A smile of recognition started with her nice forget-me-not eyes, spread to her nice pink mouth, and finally her round, plump face, with its halo of fluffy white curls, flushed with pleasure.

"You're just in time for lunch, Bill." As though he had come from down the street instead of across an ocean and a continent and a space of time that Maggie and I had carefully forgotten.

Four years ago a young man named Bill had stepped

through that same door, claimed us as aunts, and settled down for the summer. A month later he had rewarded our wholehearted hospitality by bashing in the heads of the couple next door, contriving to rob his mother, our sister, at the same time placing the blame for the murders on her, and breaking a young girl's heart. If he hadn't broken Virginia's heart, he had, at the very least, trifled with her affections.

His mother had died from the shock, and Maggie and I would, forevermore, be allergic to nephews named Bill. And this brown-eyed young giant before us now was the Bill that that other Bill had been impersonating. I shivered.

Maggie said, "When did you get out?"

"Out of bed?" Bill showed even white teeth in a grin. He lifted his brows suddenly. "Or did you mean San Francisco?"

Maggie said, "I meant everything."

I hugged him again and said, "Anyway, we're glad you're here. How long?"

"Oh!" Vaguely. "A week or two."

He seemed to sag a little in the doorway, and I thought, "The boy's sick." I pulled him over to the glider.

Maggie went into a methodical bustle that I recognized as her form of killing the fatted calf. "You two talk while I whip up a lunch. Bill, you look as though you could use a good, home-cooked meal."

Bill wilted onto the glider. He sighed aloud and from the depths, pushed a pillow into place behind his shoulders, and gave me a white smile that said, "I've come home, and this is where I want to be."

A very good place, Ogg Lake in June. A nice, warm, upstate-New York June, with schools closed and families in the cottages, blue skies, green fields, and the cottonwoods fluffing out all over the place. Harris Cove is in the middle of the east side of the lake, and the Harris house is in the middle of the cove, and the Harris sisters, Maggie and I, right where we belonged, in the middle of it all. After almost a year away it was wonderful to be home, with the whole long summer ahead. With the Johnsons on our left and the Lanes next to them. On our right the Long cottage and beyond them the Roberts.

The Longs and the Roberts we didn't see much of; our house seemed to face the other way. But the Johnsons were like our own family; they were our own: Max and Mommie and their four daughters. And Grampie. Grampie, sitting out under the cottonwoods in the warm evenings.

The Lanes. Mr. Lane a nonentity; Mrs. Lane a busy woman, the busiest woman I've ever known. Busy at nothing, busy at everything. And Virginia Lane. Virginia, who had grown up, in spite of her mother, to be a rather exceptional person. Sincere, possessing integrity, with excellent control, her only fault a tendency to be unsure of herself. Perhaps now that she was out of college and ready to start a career, she'd get away from her mother, who could confuse anyone, and perhaps that indecisiveness would leave her.

I got up from my chair and set the table on the porch. Bill's eyes were closed; he looked thin and ill. My heart twisted. We didn't know our nephew very well, not half so well as we would wish. Carrie had died when he was born, and Will, his father, had kept the boy with him; except for the war, of course. For a brief week, four years ago, Maggie and I had had him as a house guest and liked him. That was all. I looked at him again.

I saw six feet of good, straight bones covered loosely with an adequate amount of muscle and tan gabardine. I tried to imagine how he would look with twenty or thirty more pounds of flesh where it would do the most good. His cheekbones looked as though they were about to burst the skin, and that tight look around his mouth could have been acquired only in one way—the hard way. His color wasn't right. He had been deeply tanned not too long ago, tanned by a tropical sun and then bleached out rather thoroughly. We would take care of that, along with the twenty pounds, we and the sun on Ogg Lake.

I said, "Have you been sick, Bill?"

"You don't think I'm breaking in this pallor for a friend, do you?" The quick, wide smile that accompanied the remark removed any glib freshness I might have noticed, and anyway, I don't want a nephew who thinks he has to respect my gray hairs. I took the pot of tea Maggie handed me and set it on the hot pad at her place at the table.

"If you want to wash, use the lavatory off the study," I said. "Remember where it is?"

"Through here?" Bill pulled himself to his feet reluctantly, moved to the door of Papa's study, and disappeared at my nod.

Maggie and I sat down. Bill came back shortly, his face shining like a small boy's, his hair wet. He looked, at the moment, like a hungry teen-ager instead of a twenty-five-year-old. He groaned in anticipation as he sat down. A shrimp salad, watermelon pickle, and hot popovers in a napkin-covered basket. Strawberries and thick cream and a large glass of milk.

Bill favored Maggie with a look that would have melted a glacier. Maggie, who needs no melting, was reduced to fatuousness. In that one moment she became his, body and soul; Bill's doting aunt.

After the third popover Bill said, "What happened to that Johnson family next door?"

Maggie said, "The children are berrypicking, and I can hear Mommie running the vacuum cleaner. There's been a baby since you met them."

Bill said, "Max?"

Where was Max? I said, "Max started on his vacation this week, but I haven't seen him today. You see," I explained, "your aunt Maggie and I did a little tour last winter that ran over into the spring."

"We were celebrating," said Maggie. "Celebrating the sale of some city property." She gave me a look that said, "And the less said about that, the better."

Bill didn't look interested, but just in case, I said hurriedly, "That's a long story and I don't feel up to it. What Maggie means is that we haven't really seen the Johnsons since last fall."

Maggie pinched her blue eyes in a squint and tipped her head back to view the cove. "He's been right out there, been there all morning."

Bill and I followed her squint. He was. Our friend Max was enthroned in his skiff in the middle of Harris Cove. He bent over something in his lap. He seemed to be working on a board. The sun beat down unmercifully on his bare back, but his face and whatever he was doing with his hands were shaded by a large, rusty black umbrella that appeared to be stuck upright through the seat beside him. No wonder I hadn't seen him! If I had noticed the figure he made, I probably would have thought it was one of those eccentric fishermen who inhabit the shores of Ogg Lake.

Bill scraped his bowl for the last strawberry and lighted a cigarette. He refused tea, but got up and helped himself to another glass of milk. After a bit he said, "Guess I'll row out and get acquainted again. I liked that guy."

"I'll go with you," I said. "If you'll leave the dishes, Maggie," I added.

"Never fear," said Maggie. "I'll take a nap on the glider." She plumped the pillows preparatory to stretching out. "I'm curious, but not that curious. You'll get a sunstroke."

"I could use one," said Bill. He ground out his cigarette and surveyed his hands. They weren't too white, but they did look underexposed.

We got into the skiff, and I shoved off as Bill took up the oars. If Max saw us coming, he gave no sign. We drew near, and I was about to hail him when I discovered his occupation. Sheer astonishment made me open my mouth and speechlessness let it hang open. He was painting! With oils. Max Johnson! With a silly little paintbrush in his hand, he was making dabs on a canvas. I closed my mouth, swallowed, and choked.

Without taking his eyes from the board in his lap, Max said, "What's wrong with my painting a picture?"

"Nothing," I stammered. "I didn't know—you didn't say —Mommie——"

"You've been away, remember? And I don't know how —yet. But get this, you two." Max leveled a paint-stained finger in our direction. "If Abbie Harris can write a story and sell it to a publishing firm, I, Max Johnson, can paint a picture and have it hung in the Memorial Art Gallery. And I will, too." He spoke with conviction. He lowered his finger and addressed Bill. "Hello, Bill. You are Bill Hunt, aren't you?" Max carefully placed his brush upside down in a jelly glass on the floor of the skiff and shook hands over the side with the grinning Bill.

I opened and closed my mouth a few times and watched

Bill. He must think us a queer bunch. He didn't; he had a speculative expression on his face. He said slowly, "That's exactly what I want to do. That's what I'm going to do. I've decided!"

I said, "What!"

"The doc seems to think I should lie low this summer. There isn't much muscle outlay in painting, is there, Johnson?"

Max looked up quickly, with the air of one not to be taken in. He smiled agreement, seeing that Bill was in earnest, and shook his head. "Not unless you insist on painting from the top of a tree—or the bottom of a well."

"But why out here?" I waved my arms, indicating the blue water.

"Suggest me a better place."

I couldn't, so I kept still. But a small boat as a place to paint smacked of eccentricity. I finally said so.

Max turned a sharp, acrid look in my direction. He was very patient. "Have you ever tried to paint—or do anything creative—surrounded by five females, one not quite four?"

Max dismissed me and picked up a handful of brushes and dipped them into something and began cleaning them. He wiped them on what was once a baby's shirt. "Glad to see you, Bill. On vacation?"

Bill said thoughtfully, "There was a fellow in our outfit who was a pretty good dauber. Bet he'd like it here. Yes, vacation; permanent."

"I'll never get over it," I said. "What are you doing, the shore line?"

Max picked up the canvas and turned it around to face us. I closed my eyes, unbelieving, opened them swiftly again, and brought them to focus on the man himself. His face was blandly inscrutable, eyes wide and brown, mouth serious, no twitch of a smile. He must be out of his mind! Who would sit in the middle of the lake to paint a snow scene? On a hot June day! I reached a shaky hand out and pulled the skiff a bit closer. Yes, it was snow! A clearing in a forest; a log cabin, dark and primitive, with oiled skin at the window, and over it all a blanket of snow. A streak of red sunrise in the sky, the reflection touching the snow, emphasizing the shadows and the cold.

I said, "If this is what happens to painters—— Bill," I pleaded, "you can't. I won't let you!"

Bill said, "Don't get excited, Aunt, I don't own any paints yet. But I know a fellow who is looking for a place to paint. These hills—I had forgotten——" He waved an arm, indicating the steep sides of Ogg, all bright green with early summer. "Think we could get a place to stay? I half promised——"

Max was putting caps on tubes, closing cigar boxes, preparing to shut up shop for the day. The umbrella came down; that, I recognized, was a very old one of Grampie's. He pulled up the anchor and we followed him shoreward.

Mommie met us on the pier. Mommie is one of my favorite people; she has blue eyes that can change to green in a split second; she has a head of hair that is short, thick, and red, a dark chestnut red. She moves slowly and never moves unless she has to, and her voice is quick and low except when she gets excited, then it raises in tone, but fast.

Mommie's reaction to new people is a never-failing source of interest to me. She forms instant likes and dislikes for strangers, and I watched her now.

"Hello, Bill. Maggie told me you were here." She shook hands, swooping down on one knee to reach his. Not gushy or overanxious, but naturally and a little on the cautious. She liked him. Her most violent likes were always apparent in an extra-careful approach.

To Max she said, "Be sure you put that masterpiece on the plate rail so the baby doesn't get at it. And it's about time you came in; don't you want your lunch?"

"Stop rattling, hemphead." Max handed her an armful of cigar boxes. "Always gnashing her chompers, and about what? Nothing!"

Bill gave me a hand up out of the skiff. In the act of tying the boat to the pier I saw him freeze. I followed his eyes. Virginia Lane was crossing the lawn in front of the Johnsons'.

Virginia, at twenty-one, was definitely something to look at. Slender and not too tall, with beautifully straight shoulders and smooth-moving hips and pretty, long legs. A face to go with the proud, high-breasted way she carried herself, a face with nice brown eyes, a full, sweet mouth, and a lift to her chin that had been there always, even as a child. Her hair was brown.

She spoke now, her voice throaty and musical. "Hi, Johnsons. Hi, Abbie."

Bill stood up. Virginia blinked and moved swiftly toward the young man who seemed to have become permanently immobile. "Hello, Bill Hunt."

Bill became speechless as well as inert. She gave him her hand and swung it back and forth a little. "You are Bill Hunt, aren't you? Hello."

Articulation and locomotion returned simultaneously. Bill pumped her hand like a brother Kiwanis and grinned his wide white grin. "Hello, Virginia. Thank you for writing to me."

"I enjoyed your letters too." And that seemed to be the extent of their small talk. They stood and looked at each other. Max and Mommie disappeared. I went up on the porch and found Maggie making lady snores on the glider.

I heard Bill say, "You're just as I imagined you. I mean remembered."

Virginia laughed. "How long are you staying?"

I heard Bill answer, "All summer."

Well, that would be nice.

That evening, after Bill was unpacked and settled in the guest room over the porch and his blue, four-seater convertible had found a place next to Maggie's old coupé in the garage, he joined us on the porch. He had changed his gabardine slacks for dark trousers and light sports jacket.

"You know," he said, "the more I think about it, the better I like the idea."

"What idea?" asked Maggie.

"What do you think of my calling Johnny Rutland and asking him if he wants to spend the summer here? There is a hotel at the Point, isn't there?"

"Certainly, call Johnny, if you wish," said Maggie, "but don't talk about hotels. We've plenty of room here." Maggie, I knew, hadn't known about Johnny and his painting ability. I could see that Bill really rated with Maggie. How did she know but what Johnny might eat crackers in bed or harbor odd pets? She hadn't asked.

I remembered a house guest we had put up one horrible summer. She was afraid of food; it was all poison to her, she said. She wouldn't eat meat with this; she wouldn't eat vegetables with that. What was worse, she wouldn't let us. It got so that Maggie and I were taking our nourishment at night. We'd sneak down to our kitchen and gorge ourselves after we were sure she was safely asleep. Lobster

Newburg and large glasses of milk. Welsh rabbits, washed down with beer. That was the summer we gained so much.

"I'm sure," said Bill, "that Johnny wouldn't want to impose on your hospitality, Aunt. If I know the guy, he'll want to find a cottage of his own." I breathed a sigh of relief.

"Nonsense," said Maggie. "We've lots of room."

Bill shook his head doubtfully. "I don't know. Johnny's a little shaky, as I am from—— He wouldn't walk in on strangers. Couldn't we get a cottage? So that we could keep it as messy as we wished. Painters aren't neat."

Maggie frowned. "I'm sure all the cottages are rented by now, Bill. Wait a minute." Maggie leaned forward in her rocker. "If you don't think he'd stay here, there's that place in the hills. The Blue Place—on Marrowback."

Bill looked interested. "What's Marrowback?"

"Marrowback is the name of one of the hills." Maggie waved a plump arm up in no particular direction, just up. "It's vacant now—has been since last summer. You could have it."

"If Marrowback's a hill, what's the Blue Place?"

I explained. "One of the old farms that your grandfather owned. If I remember right, it has one of the prettiest views around here. You can see three lakes from the front porch."

Maggie leaned back and resumed her rocking. "No one rents it in the winter, of course. But summers—an artist rented it last, and if one artist liked it—well——"

Bill said, "Sold." He got up from the railing where he had been sitting, back to a pillar, and we heard him in Papa's study asking for long-distance. He came out in a very few minutes and threw himself into a rocker, long legs straight out in front of him.

"Jumped at it. He's bored to death where he is. He'll be here Friday. We can keep bach—and, who knows, an artist may be born." Bill winked at me. "Any talent in the family?"

Maggie said, "Mama painted china."

I said, "I color a mean Easter egg."

Bill jumped to his feet, pushed open the screen door, letting it slam behind him, and disappeared in the direction of Virginia's, whistling.

Max and Mommie sauntered over. Maggie got some beer from the icebox. Max said, "Just remembered something, Abbie. If Bill was serious, I know where he can get some very superior stuff for almost nothing. In fact, if it was legal I'd take them myself."

"If it isn't legal, Bill——" Maggie said. "We don't want——"

I said, "Explain."

Max held up his beer glass and admired the bubbles. "You know how we work it in Customs? If anything is left unclaimed or abandoned there for a year, it is put up for auction and sold."

Maggie said, "No!"

I said, "Yes?"

Max took a deep swallow. "About a year ago a set of paints came through from Europe—stuff you can't buy over here any more—stuff that will be scarce for years. I've been drooling; I'll be glad when they're gone. Little old guy who claimed them didn't have the duty with him."

Maggie interrupted. "I didn't know you handled stuff from Europe, Max. It's an inland port, our Customs, isn't it? I would suppose things from Canada—but Europe— don't they take care of that in New York or Boston?"

Max filled his glass from the bottle between his feet.

"Anything forwarded in bond to our city or mailed and valued at over a hundred dollars arrives at our office and the duty is collected by us. Now stop your irrelevancies. Where was I?"

Mommie said, "The consignee came to claim the package and he didn't have the duty. Was he an artist? Artists are always poor, especially married ones."

"Nope, a funny thing. He was a janitor. Must have had a GI son over there. They certainly picked up some queer stuff, those kids, to send home."

"Why didn't he get the money and come back?" I asked. "Usually parents break their necks for that sort of thing."

"Hit by a car, leaving the building. Dead. Accident."

Mommie said, "Yes? And——"

Max spread his hands, setting his glass on the floor. "And no one claimed it. So I told you, it's up for auction."

Maggie, the practical, said, "What was the matter with letting the son know, so he could reconsign it?"

Max moved his head slowly and brought his eyes to rest on Maggie. He closed them as if the sight hurt. "We thought of that, lady. The letter came back marked, 'No such name or number,' or something."

I said, "When?"

"When what?"

"When does this go up for auction?"

"Let's see. The thirtieth of this month."

"The thirtieth falls on a Sunday," Mommie said.

"Well, that means Monday, then."

Maggie said, "Why don't you bid on it yourself, Max? What makes you so bighearted? You could use them, couldn't you?"

Once more Max winced, and a look of pain closed his eyes and compressed his lips. "I'd give my eyeteeth for it.

No can do. There is a rule—an old Customs' custom, so to speak—that employees and their families cannot bid in on the auctions."

"Or don't you think I wouldn't have a new fur coat once in a while." Mommie sounded bitter.

"There may even be a squawk because Bill is a friend, but on the other hand, are many artists going to be there? I don't think so," Max answered himself. "If he has no competition, Bill can offer them five dollars or even one. It is not necessary that the amount of duty due be bid. Articles put up for auction go for what is bid, regardless of the amount. So start with a small amount; he'll probably get it. And it is worth well over a hundred dollars."

"Swell," I said. "How does he go about it?"

"I'll have to go in to the office Monday and take a look at the books. You or Maggie bring him in, and I'll give you a push in the right direction at the right time. And we won't get too chummy in front of the other guys."

There we left it. The next morning I explained it all to Bill and he was delighted. I looked at the thin young face across the table from me. He had a bit more color already. The clear brown eyes smiled at me in a friendly way, and I wondered if the phone call had been a nightmare. Then I saw the big nervous hands jerk uncontrollably as he put the spoon into his coffee. And I knew it had been real.

When it had rung, I had stumbled halfway down the stairs before I realized I was out of bed and in nothing but a blue jersey nightgown. I called back over my shoulder, "I'll take it, Maggie."

Into the phone I said, "Hello."

"Is that you, Alberta?"

"Yes."

"This is Will—Will Hunt."

"Why, hello! Hello, Will! Your boy got here today."

"Good! That's why I'm calling."

"Why didn't you come along?"

"How is he? Business; can't get away. How did he seem to you?"

"A little thin, but Maggie will take care of that, Will. We talked him into staying all summer."

"Good, again! He'll be in excellent hands."

"Why, thank you, Will. I didn't know you rated us so highly."

"I hated—I hesitated to let him come, Alberta. He's a sick boy. He's a lot sicker than he realizes."

"Sick!"

"Yes." Will's voice came to me clearly over the phone wires, and he sounded like a tired man, like a man with a heavy heart.

"Then—you weren't being funny?"

"Lord no! I'm not being funny. I'm serious, dead serious."

"I'm sorry, Will. Is there anything you want us to do?"

"This——" The voice faltered, and I pictured in my mind a man laying down a burden. "Hard to say, Alberta. I feel that his coming to you at a time like this is a—well—a distinct imposition."

"Nonsense! We're his family."

"He should be under the doctor's care—I couldn't keep him here—he does have a right to make some decisions—and there was the danger of doing more damage by interference—but if it was any place but yours——"

"Will! You're only confusing me! What are you trying to tell me?"

"Just that he should be kept quiet; watched fairly close——"

"What do you mean by watching—what'll I watch for?" I felt my heart pound. Phone conversations can never be too satisfactory. I wished I could see my brother-in-law's face.

He said finally, "Watch for anger signs. He is not to get angry. Alberta, as a child he had a nice, even disposition, as a young man the same, but since this head injury——"

"Will, you don't think this is permanent?"

"The doctors say not. It's a matter of repairing nerve tissue—that and keeping quiet—keeping happy, and marking time."

"This is just the place to do that, Will. Now don't you worry. Maggie and I are watching him already. He's in good hands."

"I do feel better, Alberta. How can I ever thank you? A man gets twisted sometimes in his thinking. And I had a brother who—well—I guess there isn't much to this inheritance stuff." Will laughed relievedly and hung up shortly, promising to call at least once a week for a report. I put the receiver back slowly and reluctantly.

"Yes, Maggie," I said. "It was Will. He wanted to know if Bill got here all right."

TWO

"Tell me about Johnny," I said. It was Monday morning and we were on the road to the city, Bill and I, in Bill's car. The top was down, and the road ahead dipped and rose invitingly, dappled in places by the morning sun which slanted through the roadside trees, promising the heat to follow in the bare places which looked black and sticky already. The hilly countryside rolled past us rapidly enough to make a pleasant breeze, and I could see that

Bill's world was all right, he looked happy. His face had actually filled out in a week.

He turned his head and beamed. "You and Maggie are a couple of swell eggs to turn over that place to us. When Johnny got in on Friday and I took him up on Marrowback Hill to our own Blue Place—well——" He made a clicking noise in the corner of his mouth indicative of complete bliss.

"Did he like the view?"

"Did he like the view! We can see as far south as the Pennsylvania hills and north to the big lake."

"Don't you forget those small lakes," I said.

"I know," Bill said. "We'll probably paint each and every one of them." He laughed after a moment and added, "And the glacier that was responsible."

We rolled along for a couple of miles in silence. *Will, I told myself, is crazy. This boy beside me isn't a bundle of sick nerves—he has showed no sign of abnormality. Will is an old woman!*

Aloud I said, "Kind of scantily furnished, though, your house."

"Say, not at all. We want a place to sleep, a table to eat from, and a stove to cook on. Those easy chairs are pure frivolity, folderol." Bill whistled happily and tunefully. We covered another mile.

"Maggie," I said, "won't rest until she gets those curtains up."

"We don't care. Let her play house if she wants to. Johnny and I will be too busy to notice. Why, who knows, we may end up with enough canvas covered at the close of the season to have a two-man show! Not to mention a tan."

I said again, "Tell me about Johnny."

"What do you want to know?"

"Everything."

Bill whistled thoughtfully for a moment, then he asked, "Do you like him?"

"A great deal; he's charming."

"He's tops, Abbie." Bill took one hand off the wheel and gestured enthusiastically. "I watched him paint some swell stuff over in the Pacific." He made that clicking sound again. "If I can just rub off a little of his genius—well!"

I wondered what Will would say. Was painting in oils nervous work? I'd ask Will tonight when he called. I said, "You don't want to make painting your lifework, do you?"

"Lord no! You can't be a real painter after twenty-five," Bill explained. "You have to start young." Bill tossed a hand upward, as if it had been full of years and he was throwing them over his shoulder.

I argued, "Johnny isn't so young."

"Johnny's thirty now, and he's been at it all his life. He's hardly started."

"Does he have a family?"

"Nope. Both dead. He was born somewhere in Pennsylvania, went to school in New York——"

"Married?"

"Well—he is and he isn't. Married a kid when he was still in school, and her parents fluffed that right away."

"Too bad," I said.

"Sour on women, he says, for a long time," Bill continued. "Then on a furlough in the South he married again. Three years ago."

"Well?" I said. "Why isn't he with her? Or she with him?"

Marriage, to me, has always been as simple as that. If you were married, you were together. Bill turned a superior smile in my direction. Marriage, it seems, isn't always as simple as that; that is, marriage as it was gone into in the war years.

Bill explained, managing to suggest that he'd modify the statement, keep it clean, in deference to my innocence. "Seems she took his allotment and all the money he'd send and then found someone to spend it on. The guy just ain't lucky in love! That's one reason I was glad I could steer him this way for the first little while he's home. Needs someone to be a family to him."

We reached the outskirts of the city. I directed Bill, smiling inwardly. To be protected was a new experience to me. The idea of this babe in the wood keeping the sordid side of life from his old aunt tickled my fancy, and I had trouble with a new twitch in the corner of my mouth. I sobered finally, with the mental resolve to be as much of a family to Johnny as I could manage, and I knew, from past experience, that Maggie would fuss over him, mother him. Maggie's mothering instinct is well developed and inexhaustible.

And yet, in spite of Bill's patent hero worship of the older man, I held a few reservations about Johnny's perfection. I liked the way he looked: six feet of handsome manhood; thick, black, curly hair, merry gray eyes, and a voice that was satisfactorily deep. Very smooth approach, very sure of himself, and all the superficial mannerisms of a gentleman, but——

I didn't like the way he looked at Virginia, when anyone with half an eye could see that Bill was in love with her. I didn't like the way he looked at Mommie—not but what Mommie could take care of herself; she hasn't red hair for nothing. Nevertheless, the man shouldn't ogle; at least not the females in his immediate circle of friends.

We drew up to a parking meter in front of the Federal Building. I said, "Shouldn't we put the car in a parking lot?" pointing to one adjacent.

"No," said Bill. "Max promised it wouldn't take long." He put a nickel into the meter and we climbed the long flight of steps. In the building we turned left toward Max's office. The sign above the door said, "U. S. Customs: Appraiser's Stores." I opened the door.

Max rose to his feet behind a huge desk that looked perfectly bare. Didn't he do any work? I asked him, and he ignored me, leading the way to an inner office that was larger and contained a desk that was barer, if possible. Max introduced us to his boss. I liked Mr. King; he was friendly. Bill looked around eagerly.

Mr. King said, "No, we don't keep the things in here. We're executives." He laughed heartily.

"You know!" said Max. "Rugs on the floor." He consulted his watch. At Bill's blank look he said, "Joke."

Bill said, "Oh!"

I told Mr. King that it had been a pleasure to meet him; he said the pleasure was all his and conducted us to the door.

Max said to Bill, "You're right on time. Good. We'll go downstairs and see what's on the docket." Mr. King held the door and bowed us out. We said good-by.

Mr. King opened the door again and called to Max, "Say, Johnson, see if you can get rid of that old Swiss cuckoo." His hearty laugh followed us down the hall.

We walked along to the front of the building and stopped before the elevators. People were bustling about with that early-morning businesslike manner they exhibit before noon: carrying papers to and fro, slamming doors, greeting one another with false heartiness.

There was a small knot of men manifesting a group attitude exactly opposite to the bustlers. These men struck me
as people who were going nowhere in particular; in fact,
they appeared surprised to find themselves where they
were, and a bit, not much more, surprised to find each
other. And the majority of these men looked as though they
had stepped out of their own pawnshops merely for a
matter of minutes. That is, all but one.

I was mildly surprised to see Orrin Keller, and the sight
of his full-moon face made me think of Maggie's watch.
Why hadn't I brought it along this morning? And that
lavaliere that had dropped its pendant.

"Hello, Orrin," I said. "What are you doing down here?"
I refrained from mentioning the jewelry that needed mend-
ing.

Orrin opened light eyes wide and seized my hand. "Good
morning! Good morning, dear lady. How are you?"

Orrin is a summer neighbor of ours. We have known
him, his brother George, and their respective families
perhaps thirty years, or I should say, thirty summers. He
was a big, heavy man, a little older than Maggie and me,
with an accrescent paunch, blue eyes that displayed an
insatiable curiosity about everything they took in, and a
wife whom I heartily disliked. Ever since that first day
I met the woman. It was at an afternoon lawn bridge at a
mutual friend's house on the other side of the lake. Jeannette
had been polite and interested until she had dug out the
fact that our house at the lake was an old family home-
stead and not one of the showy, newly built plaster jobs
that would look a mess in a generation. Anyone who tries
to make a Florida or a California out of one of the Finger
Lakes in New York State is either crazy or a four-flushing

climber. Jeannette Keller was both, and I felt sorry for
Orrin, having to spend his adult life trying to satisfy her.

I gave him my warmest smile. "Fine," I said.

"Why didn't you say you were coming to the city? I
could have dropped you off as well as not. Did you drive?"
Orrin petted the hand he still held.

A little stuffy, Orrin. A little on the prim side. But then
that stuffy, prim mannerism may have been protective
coloring. Orrin and George Keller were partners in a very
successful jewelry business in the city. Their properties,
side by side on the opposite side of Ogg Lake, were show
places. The brothers Keller might be human down underneath—they both had grown families; George had two
grandchildren—but as far as I could see, they were merely
fronts. Like their big summer homes, like the plate-glass
and chromium establishment in the city. Sometime, I
promised myself, I'd ply them with strong drink and soft
words and see if—well, just see!

"Thank you, Orrin," I said, and disengaged my hand. "I
drove, or rather my nephew did." I turned to indicate Bill.
He had disappeared! No doubt he and Max were already
on the elevator. Dogs! Couldn't they wait for a lady?

"I didn't know you had a nephew," Orrin said, and
wished he hadn't.

He remembered that I had a nephew. I saw the remembrance color his face now, a painful, embarrassed red. I
said, hastily and too brightly, "Oh, I have a nephew. You'll
probably see a lot of him; he's with us for the summer." I
started for the elevator.

Orrin took my arm chummily, to show he didn't remember, or, if he did, it mattered not at all, and turned with me
to the door. At that moment a man in a soldier's uniform
touched his sleeve. Orrin turned at the touch and I fled.

The elevator door shut and we shot downward. I gave Bill and Max a look that should have withered them on the vine.

We came out into the basement hall and entered a door to the right. Max introduced us to a man named Monroe: he called him Juke.

Juke consulted his watch and said, "Got to make this legal. Auction starts at nine. Where is everyone?"

Max said, "Seems to have hit a bottleneck upstairs."

Bill went, like a steel bar to a magnet, straight to a table and lifted a brown-paper-wrapped package. He looked around questioningly. "This?"

Juke said, "What you interested in?"

"Paints," said Bill.

"That's it," said Juke. "Go right ahead and look at them."

I moved over beside Bill. He removed the wrapper, released the little brass catch with a thumbnail, and lifted the lid on the polished walnut box. The inside was sectioned off with wooden partitions and housed perhaps fifty fat tubes of paint, together with two extra-large tubes of flake white, two bottles of turpentine and linseed oil, and a half dozen brushes. A palette fit into the cover. I chuckled, thinking of Max and his cigar boxes. Bill looked like a kid with new skates.

He said, "How much?"

Juke said, "What's the appraisal?"

Bill turned the package over, searching. "One hundred and ten dollars."

"What'll you give me?"

The answer came quickly. "Eleven dollars."

"Sold," said Juke, "to the man in the light blue sports shirt; wrap it up."

Bill laid the package down and dug into his pocket.

I examined the other exhibits. Some very nice Italian embroidery and some costume jewelry that looked heavy and old and oriental. Oodles of that. Some South American woven things and some Mexican pottery. In addition there was some uninteresting dusty machinery. I turned back to the Mexican pottery.

Bill didn't give me a chance. "Come on, let's go, Aunt." He was out the door, hugging his bundle, and I was forced to follow.

Orrin stepped off the elevator, deep in conversation with his soldier friend and surrounded by what Max calls the First Street Regulars. He turned his head and gave me a salute as the elevator door closed on our return trip.

Bill dragged me to three art-supply stores and spent considerable on incidentals. Pencils, canvas, turpentine, more and varied brushes, charcoal, and, finally, an easel.

"Max," he explained, "will laugh. But let him. I'm saving so much on that paint that all this other stuff is practically gratis." And if that wasn't Papa coming out in his grandson, I don't know heredity when it is related to me!

We ate lunch before we left the city, so it was two o'clock before we got back to the lake. Mommie and Maggie were out on the lawn between the two cottages, setting each other's hair. Bill bounded out of the car and immediately spread his purchases on the grass before the women.

Mommie examined the tubes of paint. "So this is what Max has been so hot and bothered about for a year. Don't look any different from the ones he buys."

"They are," said Bill. As if he knew! He was quoting, I was certain.

Mommie said, "You'll be lucky if he doesn't hit you on the head for the stuff."

Maggie admired things in her mild, motherly way. "My, my! They're beautiful. You had a caller this noon."

I said, "I?"

"No; Bill. A blonde."

"A blonde," said Bill. "I don't know any blondes."

"Why didn't you keep her for lunch?" I queried.

Maggie said, "I wanted her to stay, but she wouldn't. We had had ours. We didn't know if you were coming back here or going straight up to the Blue Place."

"So we drew a map," said Mommie.

"What'd she look like?" Bill started to rewrap his packages. "And why a map?"

Maggie and Mommie exchanged glances quickly. I frowned, puzzled. Maggie rolled her blue eyes and then closed them. She said, "So she could find the Blue Place."

Mommie hesitated, biting her lower lip. "Young and married. At least, she wore a wedding ring. She drove a sedan with a Texas license."

"Texas! I don't know anyone in Texas."

"Past catching up with you?" I teased.

"You're making it up," said Bill. "I'm going to show Virginia." He picked up his treasures and started toward the Lane cottage.

Mommie stopped him with a gesture. Again between Mommie and Maggie there was that exchange of glances. Mommie said, "Virginia's gone."

"Gone? Gone where?"

Maggie said hastily, "Johnny came down for lunch and took Virginia back with him for the afternoon. Guess they expected you to be there."

Mommie said, "They'd just left when the blonde came."

Bill stood stock-still for a long minute, arms loaded with

brown-paper parcels, forehead creased in thought. He
wheeled in his tracks and made for his car. Over his shoulder he said, "So long." The car tore out of the driveway and
roared up the road toward the hills.

Mommie said, "Forgot to tell him about our plans for a
picnic at the Blue Place tomorrow. Oh well, Virginia'll——"

That evening I joined Grampie out under the cottonwoods to watch the sunset. It was a common, ordinary, run-
of-the-mill sunset, but we enjoyed it. The lake was very
still, glassy-smooth, reflecting both the streaks of red left
in the darkening sky and the lights winking on across the
lake. Surprisingly, there were no boats to be seen. Grampie
got the thought just as it occurred to me.

"Might as well enjoy this quiet while we can. After
Thursday, things will be popping for the rest of the summer."

"Is Thursday the Fourth?"

"Sneaks up on you, doesn't it, Abbie?"

I said, "Oh! Well, if the Fourth comes quickly, so will
Labor Day. After that, things quiet down." That took care
of that. We smoked in companionable silence for perhaps
half an hour.

The first intimation I had that we were no longer alone
was the dip of an oar near us and a bump against the dock.
I got up. Two men were getting out of a boat and walking
the length of our dock.

It was Orrin Keller. I should have known. He is the only
person on our lake with an electric boat. A beautiful job
that is perfectly silent in operation. Uncanny, the way it
moves through the water, seeming to be on top, rather than
in the water.

I said, "Good evening."

"Good evening, Abbie, good evening. Where's everyone? Your sister?"

Right away a question! I said, "Out. I didn't ask her where she was going. It is a nice evening."

"Perfect. Perfect." He turned to his companion, the young man in uniform. "This is Frank Sorbus, Abbie. Miss Harris, Frank. Do you remember each other?"

I looked closer. Remember Frankie Sorbus? Of course I did! He had been one of the big boys I taught my first year; eighth grade. That would make him—let's see, I had been twenty—he must be thirty-six or thirty-eight by now.

Orrin was buzzing along, happily, with his story. "Frank used to work for me before the Army got him. He's just back after twenty-five months, and I'm darn glad to get him. Nothing's worked right since he's been gone."

I said cordially, "Good evening, Frank. I'm glad to see you."

Frankie's voice, husky, muffled, seemed to be coming from almost anywhere except his lips. I wondered if he was practicing ventriloquism. I'm sure his lips didn't move. He approached me sidewise, raising and lowering his eyebrows rapidly.

"Good evening, Miss Harris."

"Ran into a little trouble right in front of your place," explained Orrin Keller. "Thought maybe you'd have a screwdriver."

Frankie shot his eyebrows up again and then let them down. I found Grampie at my elbow. Orrin said, after the greeting, "My own fault. Shouldn't let so many people use the boat."

Grampie said, "I'll see what I can find in the car." He was back in a moment with a kit which he handed to Frank Sorbus. "Anything else?"

"Nope." Frankie disappeared into the depths of the boat. We started shoreward.

"Thank you, no," said Orrin Keller. "I'll join you while he tinkers. Born tinkerer."

We walked back to the lawn chairs under the trees and sat down. I knew what Grampie and I were in for: a quiz. Orrin Keller should be on the radio. I sent a mental invocation dockward: "Please, Frankie, be a fast tinkerer."

Orrin said, "How are all your folks, Doctor?"

"Fine."

"Where is everyone?"

"The children are in bed, and Max and my daughter are down at the Point."

"Just a sitter, eh?" Orrin laughed artificially, irritating me more than the witticism should have. I suppose a man who meets the public daily gets into the way of talking a formula. His manner of leaning across a jeweler's showcase never left him. I always had the feeling, when talking to Orrin, that he was showing me something beautiful and it left him breathless. I invariably found myself getting breathless too.

Grampie said nothing and offered us his cigarettes. Orrin refused and in turn offered Grampie a cigar. "Thank you, Keller. Isn't often I get to smoke a banker's cigar." He lighted it slowly, savoring the first draw. "This is all right."

A flashlight out on the boat moved around.

Orrin lighted the mate to Grampie's cigar and after a few puffs held it out at arm's length and admired the red glow on the end. He said, "Ran into Abbie today, and of all places, in the Federal Building. Of all places. Trouble with your income tax, Abbie?"

I said, "No. I was with Bill."

"Bill, your nephew?"

"Yes."

"Can't get over your having a—a nephew." He had been on the point of saying another nephew. I bristled. "Which one of your sisters does he belong to?"

"Carrie," I said shortly.

"I remember her. She was more my age than yours, wasn't she?"

"Yes."

"What's he doing in the Federal Building? Looking for a job?"

"No," I said. I was mad enough to leave it there, and then my sense of humor got the better of me and I thought, "What's the use. He's going to get it out of me anyway, and why give Grampie——" I was sharing the long seat with Grampie, and I could feel his side quiver with suppressed laughter. So I told all.

Orrin was interested, but then Orrin would be interested in the mildest trip to the grocery store. Grampie's side stopped quivering and he puffed at his cigar contentedly. I resolved to sidetrack Orrin, if it was humanly possible, and I searched my mind for a subject that would make Grampie uncomfortable. My mind was a blank, unfortunately.

Orrin said, "Nice to have the young folks about. Mrs. Keller and I try to keep the young folks near us as much as we can. What's he painting, water scenes?"

I explained about Bill and his friend Johnny Rutland and the Blue Place on Marrowback. Orrin knew the place; the artist who had rented it the summer past had been a friend of his. I turned the conversation over to Grampie by the simple procedure of mentioning Max's prowess in that direction.

Grampie, the old smoothie, took care of himself. He said, "What were you doing in the Federal Building, Keller?" I looked at Grampie in amazement. It hadn't occurred to me to turn the tables.

Orrin made a gesture of disgust. "Heard about some Italian costume jewelry coming up. George thought one of us should look it over. Worst bunch of junk I ever saw. How they have the nerve to foist——" He stood up.

"How's it coming, Sorbus?"

"Done."

They left.

THREE

On Tuesday we went up to the Blue Place for our picnic. Mommie made a crock of beans, and Virginia baked a cake. Maggie produced a potato salad and a baked ham. Max took care of the beer department. Grampie was to follow as soon as he could get away from the office. The two oldest Johnson girls had very important dates on the other side of the lake. We took the baby and the little girl with us.

The party wasn't an unqualified success.

Max had left early in the morning to get in some sketching with the boys, and the rest of us started right after lunch. We drove up the haunted-house road and over the hogback and then along the ridge, till we turned off at the sign that said "Dead End" to climb the Marrowback. It isn't far from the cove if you walk or as the crow flies, but by road it is perhaps two miles or three. And most of those miles climb upward. The Blue Place is on the highest point of those hills, and the old one-track road leading off the ridge is unimproved. The original owner of the place must have been not so much a farmer as a lover of beauty, for the hills are too steep to cultivate successfully. It isn't stony country; on the contrary, it is very fertile and thickly wooded, where the owners haven't cut the trees down.

We wound our way upward in the ruts of the single track. Virginia said, "I asked the boys, yesterday, what they'd do if they met a car."

Maggie smiled. "Never met a car yet, and I've been coming here twenty years."

We reached the top and came out of the shady maple gloom to the clearing. No one was about. The old farmhouse stood alone and deserted. Blue Horizon. You certainly did come up into the blue when you traveled there. I had forgotten who had bothered to paint the little old house that heavenly blue color; I tried to remember. It hadn't lasted long: blue is a color that doesn't stand weather. It had faded in the sun and rain and wind of the years until now it was hardly more than a shadowy gray.

It was one of those farmhouses that were built by the score a hundred years ago. Facing east, the building consisted of three parts: a center that set back to shelter a doorway and a small porch; two wings that jutted out like those of a setting hen. Two little dormers in the center made it look more like a brooder every time I approached.

A driveway swung up the last rise in the ground to the doorway and then down to complete a circle and lead out again. On the opposite side of the circle stood what was left of a barn. The tenants who had painted the house hadn't thought it necessary to paint the barn, and it was a nice silvery color that blended into the slope like a lichen on a rock.

We piled out of the car, the children immediately racing to the barn and Maggie right after them.

Mommie, Virginia, and I went up to the house. It was empty. Three cars stood outside. We carried the food inside and explored. The old kitchen, which was the center room, looked desolate, unused, bare. No curtains yet. Maggie would take care of that. She insisted on putting up the old dotted-swiss ruffled curtains she found in the attic. There they lay, over a kitchen chair where the boys had dropped them. On the table were a few clean dishes. We placed our crocks and casseroles beside them. I went into the room to the right.

This was the room with the view. Our artist tenants of a few years back had put in a large picture window to the east and had taken out the partitions that had closed off two bedrooms, making one large room of the three. There were two small windows to the left and to the north. The furnishings were sparse.

The two cots that Maggie and I had provided were against the west wall, one to a window. I reminded myself to speak to the boys about that. They shouldn't, either one of them, lie under a window, even on a hot summer night.

There were two easy chairs, one on either side of the picture window, with a low, wide table between. I smiled to myself. That table had been the talk of the hills when our artists had paid two dollars for it, and then, instead of using it for a dining table, they had lowered it by sawing off the center pedestal, painted it black, and proceeded to decorate it with hearts and flowers. I liked it. Besides those necessities the room contained a wardrobe trunk, which served as a dresser, and a steamer trunk, both of which belonged to Johnny.

I crossed the room in order to shut the top tray of the wardrobe trunk; I'm the neat type. Maggie would have laughed. My one claim to neatness is that obsession of mine: I cannot stand half-open drawers. With my hand on the tray I paused. That ugly object on top of the socks looked like a gun. It was a gun!

Now, Johnny had a right to possess a gun; he was of age! But a nagging, uneasy feeling developed somewhere in my middle. A gun and a nervous, combat-fatigued boy shouldn't share the same house, let alone the same room.

I could take Johnny aside and tell him that Bill's father worried—that Bill was—that—— I snapped the tray shut. I found, upon examining my mind, that there was nothing concrete to tell. I'd mind my own business and go on, as if no gun existed, surveying this bachelor heaven Johnny and Bill had created for themselves.

"Playing hard to get?" asked Mommie.

"Personally, I think they're sleeping." Maggie selected a cushion from one of the cots and started down the drive. We followed her through the barnyard and on down the slope to the old orchard. We could hear the children in the stalls playing some sort of game that included cries of "Whoa, Nellie." I was sorry, for their sakes, that there wasn't a strawstack in the stable yard to slide down.

We found the men lying on their backs under an old, old tree and facing downhill. No wonder they hadn't heard us. They were as protected from the road as if there had been a stone wall.

Bill and Johnny had on blue T shirts and the usual gabardine slacks, their feet in woven sandals. Max wore his shorts, which were, in reality, colorless, washed-out slacks that he had cut off for himself presumably with a bread knife. His feet were decorated with a disreputable old pair of sneaks.

I cried, "What are you doing?"

Max rolled over on one elbow, indicating the world beyond and below with a lazy wave of his hand. "Soaking up atmosphere; admiring the view."

"Is that necessary?" Mommie pointed a slender finger in the direction of a neighboring apple tree. Situated on the north side, where the shade was deepest, was a large wooden pail containing beer in bottles up to their necks in what, I presumed, was well water.

"That, my fran, is what is known as the old oaken bucket. You cannot run a farm without an old oaken bucket. Or can you?"

Johnny and Bill leaped to their feet, apologetically dashed immediately to the old oaken bucket, both talking at once. Bill said, "We didn't hear you drive in."

Johnny said, "Welcome to Blue Horizon."

Max said to Mommie, "Stop twisting my arm. I'm getting up." He groaned loudly, crawling painfully to his feet, grasping the tree trunk for support. He muttered to himself, "What are they trying to do? Show me up? It's only old Harris and Lane and Johnson!"

I sank to the ground and accepted a bottle of beer. Maggie sat beside me, and Mommie moved over to the tree near Max. That young man promptly crumpled to the grass and laid his head in his wife's lap, holding his hand up weakly for his beer. She gave him the half-empty bottle, and he held it to the light, measuring the contents suspiciously.

Johnny said, "Bill and I ran into Old Village and bought glasses for the gals this morning."

Bill dipped a hand down into the bucket. "And I thought to cool a couple of cokes for you, Ginnie."

Virginia thanked him. Maggie said, "Did you wash them? The glasses, I mean." Max snorted.

Mommie poured a little of her beer on her husband's chest. She said, "What kind of a start did you make, Bill?"

Bill took his eyes away from Virginia and said, "Just a little charcoal, so far. I'm going to do the barn from this side." He gestured. "That'll give me the hill for a background." Immediately he went back to looking at Virginia.

Virginia, hair pulled up on top of her head and tied with a blue ribbon, was good to look at. Blue shorts today and a striped knit shirt that hid none of her curves, blue socks and saddle shoes at the ends of those lovely, long legs. She hitched herself up on a tree stump, tipped the coke bottle and drank, managing to look lovely in that unlovely pose.

Johnny obviously thought her easy on the eyes. His, I noticed, had taken on a glitter that made them black. He edged as close to the girl as he could decently get, his long, muscular body bent toward her in a crouch that brought his black curly head close to her ear. He said something in his deep voice that was all chest tones, something that made Virginia frown.

I saw storm signals in Bill's face. Straight brows pulled down to his nose to form a V. What had Will said a week ago? "Watch him for signs of anger." Watch him? All right, then what? Sit there on the grass and feel my heart turn to water and then freeze solid with fear? And only last night I had told Will that everything was fine!

Virginia slid down from the stump she was sitting on and said, "I'm going to find the baby. Couldn't we put up a swing?"

Max groaned again, and Johnny caught Virginia's hand and pulled her toward the barn. "I think I saw some rope in the stable; looked all right, too."

Bill sat down near me. I didn't look at him. I didn't have to. The white-hot anger in the boy emanated an aura that I felt, instinctively, would blind the looker.

Virginia came back and held out a hand. "Come on, Bill. Help us." He got up immediately and went with her toward the barn. We could hear the children greet them with cries of joy.

Mommie said, "Hey, what have we? A triangle on our hands for the summer?"

"If we have," Maggie said slowly, "I promise you someone will have to get rid of Johnny. I won't have it!" She meant it.

Max said, "Aw, the guy's all right. And Virginia is old enough to take care of herself."

Perhaps Virginia was old enough to take care of herself. But was Bill? I wondered. And I was to find out.

Bill was put on the rack that sunny afternoon and did absolutely nothing to defend himself. He put up no battle at all, no defense, and, without being obvious, I don't see how Virginia could have done differently. Johnny was just too smooth and subtle an operator. I, for one, never want to witness again such a deliberate exhibition of excoriation. I hope I never again see the life sucked out of a boy as it was drained out of Bill that day. His brown eyes took on a tortured look that was animal-like, helpless, numb. I wanted to cry out, "Do something, Bill. Don't let that guy get away with this!"

No one pretended to paint. We looked over what had been accomplished in the morning. Johnny had sketched in a rutted road between two grassy banks; a road that led the observer down a hill and out into the wilds and away from the horizon that lay beyond two drifts of forest-covered foothills. Already his sky had taken on that summer blueness with billowy clouds that made you want to lie on your back and watch them drift by. We praised it.

Max's canvas showed a section of the old rail fence that bounded the property, zigzagging over the hilltop and down. He was probably a bit behind Johnny, but not much.

Poor Bill! I knew after the first quick glance at the charcoal sketch that he would never be an artist. My heart ached for him. On the other hand, what had ever made him think he could paint? It was too precise: his canvas looked like an architect's drawing, a blueprint; too exactly to scale ever to develop into a product of the imagination.

Maggie said so. Max gave her an argument. He said that a drawing should be exactly to scale. Johnny took Maggie's side.

I lifted the cover from Bill's new box of paints. I admired it; it was beautifully finished. Inside, it hadn't been touched. It looked as though he hadn't even lifted a tube out. The brushes unused, the cups and palette knife unsoiled. I went back to his easel.

Johnny's too-amused expression when we were comparing canvases made me want to slap him. He closed one eye, bringing that corner of his mouth up in a half-smile. Virginia walked away.

Grampie arrived around six. It was shady on that side of the hill now. We laid out the picnic in the old orchard where the easels were set up. We hailed Grampie with an exuberance that couldn't have rung true. After the first five minutes of uncomfortable hilarity, Grampie's expression had run the gamut from puzzlement to comprehension, and I could see that he had the situation well placed. The children alone fell on the food with gusto. Bill ate nothing at all.

Later Maggie started to scrape the dishes. "Let's go home; it's getting cool."

I said nervously, "You wouldn't think that a little height would make all that difference."

"Two thousand feet she calls a little height!" Max was indignant. "Some people would call this a mountain." He folded up his easel, slapping the covers down on his cigar boxes.

Bill closed the clasp on his new acquisition slowly and carried it to the trunk of his car. He lifted the trunk lid, placed the new walnut case there, and lowered the cover. His canvas and easel he carried inside the house and set up again in the large room. He moved like a mechanical man. Why? He simply did not know what he was doing. The boy was blind with misery, and somehow I felt to blame. Was this the way I was taking care of him?

We stood in front of the house finally, everything packed. Maggie said, "Bill."

He looked at her soberly. "Yes?"

"Bill, you haven't told us if the blonde caught up with you."

"No, she hasn't," he said shortly.

Mommie said, "Perhaps she couldn't follow the map we gave her."

"Map?" Virginia frowned. "Are you talking about—do you mean the girl who followed us up here yesterday? Remember, Johnny?"

Johnny gave no answer, and I saw his gray eyes dart sharply from Virginia's golden-brown face to Bill's white and sick-looking one and then back to Virginia's.

She said, touching Bill's arm, "There was someone—a blonde—here looking for you yesterday. We forgot to tell you, didn't we, Johnny?"

"Did she say what she wanted?"

Virginia took her hand from Bill's arm, chilled by his expression. "I didn't talk to her."

"Then how do you know she wanted me?" Bill was rude; his voice rough with all the anguish, all the torment of the long afternoon.

Virginia lifted her head. She said stiffly, "I was already in the house when she drove up. I stood in the big window"—she gestured toward the living room—"and I'm sorry, I couldn't hear—so I couldn't say—I'm not sure——"

Bill made a quick, apologetic movement toward Virginia. The rest of us stirred uncomfortably. Why didn't Johnny speak up? He merely looked handsome, aloof, very pleased with himself.

Virginia continued haltingly, and I felt she was very near to tears. "Johnny was outside—he talked to her."

Johnny moved to Virginia's side and ran his fingers up into her hair and the back of her head. He took a firm grip and tipped her head back, turning her face to his. He smiled down at her, saying nothing. His whole gesture, his body stance was primitive, deliberately male. His smile said, "Wench, I'll deal with you when I get you alone, and you'll like it."

"Johnny!" She twisted out of his grasp and tidied her hair self-consciously.

Bill spun toward Johnny, glad to have a grievance into which to sink his teeth. I could see the relief, the release of pent-up emotion in the rage-white face. Here was something to start on. He couldn't say, "What are you hanging around my girl for?" but he could say, "Why didn't you give me the message?" and he did.

"Explain, Rutland!" He took an aggressive step nearer. His voice contained all the pent-up resentment of that

warm and miserable afternoon, all the suspicions and
doubts that must have taken root in his mind as early as
yesterday, when he had gotten back from the city and
found Johnny and Virginia gone to the hills. He repeated
roughly, "Explain."

Johnny made a single downward gesture with his hand.
"Now calm down, sonny. You'll blow your top!" He
smiled that same one-sided smile and took a pack of cigarettes out of his shirt pocket, but in spite of his non-
chalance, he took a backward step.

Grampie said, "Who's going to ride with me?" Without
a word the girls piled in, and Grampie called out to the
rest of us, "See you at the cove."

Mommie and Max moved toward their car. Bill pulled
his lips into a thin line across set teeth, and after a moment that dragged he filled the gap between himself and
Johnny and repeated softly, quietly, "Explain."

Johnny took the cigarette out of his mouth, spread his
hands, and opened his eyes very wide. A lock of hair fell
onto his forehead and lay there in a black curl. He tossed
his head. "Don't get excited, little boy. She wouldn't give
me her name. She'll look you up when it's more con-
venient, no doubt. I told her you were all dated up that
afternoon."

Virginia walked toward the cars. "May I ride with you,
Mommie?"

Bill stopped her. "You're riding with me, Virginia. I'm
going down to the cove."

Johnny's gray eyes slid sidewise to Virginia, and he
winked slowly and firmly, the rest of his face deadpan.
Max and Mommie were in the car by then and didn't see
it. Maggie saw it, and Virginia, if she did, gave no sign,
unless the color in her cheeks was a sign. That, I rather

thought, came from the tone of Bill's voice. She moved firmly to the Johnson car.

Bill watched Johnny, and that wink was the spark that touched off the fuse of his anger. He backed a step, flexed his leg muscles, feeling the ground with the balls of his feet, and swung his fist in a sudden thrust that, had Johnny not seen it and ducked in the last split second, must have sent him sprawling.

Even then Johnny looked unruffled. He spoke quickly, lifting that lock of hair with a head toss. "Listen! I'm not going to get mixed up with you when I know the shape you're in. Calm down. Can I help it if your women chase you?" He put the cigarette into his mouth again, drew deeply, and blew a cloud of smoke into the evening air.

Bill wheeled away, strode to his car, climbed over the door in one swift movement, turned the key in the ignition, pressed the starter, and drove furiously up over the lawn around both Maggie's and Max's cars and down the lane at a breakneck, drunkenly crooked pace that frightened me. I felt sick, remembering his father's conversation.

Maggie and I slept little Tuesday night. At least we told each other so at breakfast. Of course we may have been mistaken, for neither one of us had heard the door open and close, nor the stairs creak. Nothing.

We discussed the previous day. Maggie felt that this summer was going to be one of our mistakes. She said, "I'm going to find some way to eliminate Johnny. He's not good for Bill." I agreed and moved over to the glider to read the morning paper. Maggie went into the kitchen.

My heart wasn't in it. It was with relief that I laid the paper down and turned around to investigate a peculiar scrabbling sound at the Johnsons'. It was Max. He was crawling out from under his porch. I called over, "What in the world are you doing? Looking for something?"

He dragged out a large, once-red oilcan. "Told the boys I had an extra five-gallon can. And I'm looking for a sickle. They want to clear a patch out to the little house in the rear. Seems that up to now they have been forced to wear hip boots. Thistles and burdocks."

"I think there's one in the boiler room," I said. "I'll look."

There was, and I took it out to the car that Max was backing out of his garage. "Where," he asked, "is the whetstone to go with this?"

I looked blank. He said, "Never mind." He climbed out and disappeared into his garage.

I stood there, hand on the door, thinking of Bill. His desolate face had haunted me all night. I climbed into the front seat and announced, when Max got back, "I'm going along."

We didn't talk. It was probably ten o'clock, and the hills were already hot and dusty with sun. I knew that when we arrived at the top of Marrowback it would be cool, there was bound to be a breeze. I thought of the holiday ahead of us.

The Fourth of July brings so many crazy people to the cottages, all trying to crowd a summer's fun into the few days at their disposal, that we, the regular lakers, try to get away if we can. I wondered if the answer to Maggie's and my breakfast question didn't lie in a three-day-visit to Blue Horizon. If we two women couldn't freeze out one young man in that length of time—well, it was a thought and worth a try.

We turned in at the Dead End sign and started the last

climb. Just before the break in the tree-shaded gloom we almost ran into Johnny's car. Max stopped.

"Well," I said intelligently.

"Bet he ran out of gas," said Max. "Want to walk up to the house from here?"

"No," I said, pointing. "It looks as though someone plowed around him once. Can't we?"

There was a well-defined track that had swerved and gone to the left of Johnny's car. Max grunted.

"Probably Bill," I said, relieved. So Bill had gone back and spent the night at Blue Horizon. And Maggie and I had pictured him dead in a ditch! A load lifted from somewhere in the region of my middle.

Max said, "Wonder why we didn't meet him?"

I said, "He probably isn't up yet."

Max swerved well to the right and drove around Johnny's car. It wasn't easy; the undergrowth was luxuriant. In a few minutes we pulled up in the circular driveway in front of the house. Max shut off the ignition and climbed out.

"How can they sleep with that sun pouring in?" I was thinking aloud.

Max reached in the back seat and took out the oilcan. He handed me the sickle and whetstone and led the way up the path. He opened the kitchen screen and held it for me.

I called, "Yoo-hoo." I walked through the kitchen to the big room and laid the sickle on the low table. "Why, they're both gone," I started to say, when something behind me and a little to the right caught my eye. Something bulky and blue on the floor. I whirled.

It was Johnny.

Max set the red can down on the floor inside the doorway and said, "Cr—rist!"

Someone was screaming. Screaming and screaming and
screaming. It bounced back from the surrounding hills
and doubled with the new screams. It was I.

FOUR

There is a limit to the time a given female can scream; I
reached that limit eventually. The reverberations died; my
breath, coming in deep sobs, slowed, shuddered, and after
what seemed an infinity, but in reality could have been no
more than a brief moment, I controlled it once more.

Max waited, watching me. When it was over he knelt
swiftly beside Johnny and touched his shoulder and as
quickly recoiled. Johnny lay crumpled in a drear, depress-
ing heap, as if he had been knocked violently against the
wall just inside the door. There was a small soaking of
blood on the back of his blue gabardine sports shirt. The
black hair lay in ringlets, pathetically childlike above the
openmouthed, expressionless face. I wanted to brush back
that familiar lock; it made him so defenseless.

I had found a kitten once in just that state of dead un-
wantedness. A farmer had thrown the newborn pariah
against a stone wall to kill it and had let it lie there where
it had fallen.

Max's eyes met mine, and I was grateful that he said
nothing about my loss of control; I'd have resented any
comforting he might have offered me. He regarded me
thoughtfully. "Why don't you go out to the car?"

"Not till you do." My voice was someone else's, someone with a thickened, scream-torn throat.

"I'll be right here."

I shook my head dumbly and stubbornly. My stomach pulled together in a hard, cold lump. I had to ask a question. "Bill?"

Max spread his hands in a hopeless gesture and got to his feet with a single, muscle-controlled movement. He stood where he was, not moving. I remembered and followed his example, watching him, deliberately unfocusing my look so that the blue bundle at our feet was a bulky blur. Max began at the door and moved counterclockwise with his eyes. He could no more refrain from being professional in anything he did than he could stop one logical thought from tripping on the heels of another. And Max had the uncommon faculty of being able to work both ways from a situation; a posteriori and a priori; cause to effect— effect to cause—it made no difference to that brain.

Johnny's legs were bent, one under the other, his arms up and his face to one side. There was a hole in the plaster above him, a hole with a small rayed area around it.

Max let his eyes move to the window, the large window that overlooked the hills to the south. Mine followed. It was streaked and spattered with ribbons of paint! Red-orange-yellow-green-blue-violet ran through my head, horribly, irrelevantly. Underneath was a welter of split and squeezed paint tubes! Dribbles of half-dried oil color lay in worms over the two large easy chairs and defaced the table between.

Someone had run amok, gone berserk. Someone had been angry, hated Johnny. Hated him enough to kill him. And the destruction of Johnny's property had been an afterthought; wanton, vengeful spite. I felt the lump that was my stomach soften, uncurl, and wave slightly along the edges like some deep-sea, boneless thing flopping around under my ribs.

I whispered, again in the unfamiliar, hoarse voice,
"Bill." This time it wasn't so much a question as a statement.

Max still said nothing. He turned a straight-lipped,
rigidly controlled face to the side of the room opposite the
door. Under the windows there, Johnny's trunks had been
literally torn apart. The two boxes that had held his painting equipment were shattered and spilled. More slit,
squeezed, and mutilated tubes of paint had been thrown
in a rage against the walls, on the floor.

I had to turn slightly now to follow Max as he raked
the third wall with those deep-set gimlet eyes. The two
cots, obviously, hadn't been slept in. But the clothing that
had been hung overhead and behind the door had been
torn down and subjected to the same indignity the other
personal things had.

I turned back to the doorway, not moving my feet, and
gazed at Max. He avoided my look. My stomach hardened
again, settling heavily. I swallowed. "What are we going
to do?"

"You are going to get the best lawyer you know. Right
now we are going to town and——"

I swallowed again, audibly. "Couldn't it have been——"
I pleaded. "Couldn't he have——"

"Suicide?" Max helped me.

I let out my breath, snatching at the word. "Yes! Suicide!"

Max was silent, his head moving in the negative, his
expression sympathetic.

I argued. "He was unhappily married—he had been
hurt in the Pacific—he'd——"

"No gun," said Max. It was a statement that made it
final.

"Of course he had a gun!" I was pleased that Max had thought of that. "All the boys have guns—they all brought them home from the war with them. He must have had a gun! All the boys brought back guns. Bill has——"

That had been the wrong thing to say. The head was moving in that side-to-side movement that meant no, but I didn't give up. I said, "You haven't looked."

"I don't have to. It would be in plain sight."

My mind raced in circles. Where had I seen—— It came to me suddenly. "Insurance!" I cried. That was it. I read where a man rigged up a method of getting rid of the gun for insurance.

I could see that I hadn't convinced him, but he was startled. He frowned. "How——"

"Through a trap door in the ceiling of his garage. It knocked off a pot of geraniums, and that is the way the police traced the path of the gun. Elastic." I felt triumphant. Our eyes swept to the ceiling simultaneously. No trap door. Rough old plaster with river like cracks making a relief map of it. Paint peeling with age. I curled up inside. Something gave way; something I had hung on to slipped away and left me.

Max said, "No geraniums."

I said, "What now? Sheriff?"

"I don't think so. Chief of police, Troy Ingram." Max moved to the kitchen and I followed. He turned back at the door and surveyed the room again. He said, more to himself than to me, "He probably stood over by those cots. The cartridge case will probably be in those covers. There was no fight, definitely no fight. Johnny surprised someone."

I said, "Surprised them doing what?"

"I don't know."

I went out onto the porch. The hot sunshine seemed
unreal and somehow indecent. Things shouldn't look the
same when a boy has died. I was shaking like a leaf.

Max followed me. "Did you say that Bill spent the night
here?"

"I said so—but——"

"How do you know?"

"I don't," I answered heavily. "I only know he wasn't
at the cove last night; he didn't come home." I seemed,
somehow, to be reliving some familiar situation—vaguely
—as in a dream. I said plaintively, "I worry, Max."

Max climbed behind the wheel. I got in on the other
side. I started to cry a little. Max turned on the ignition
and pressed the starter. He let out the clutch.

I said, "Can't you do something?"

We rolled down the slope and braked to a stop. "I
couldn't," he said with sad finality. "I want nothing to do
with this, Abbie."

"You—you've got to." I blew my nose.

"No. Absolutely no." Max meant it. "You get that
lawyer. Call Bill's father." He started the car again and
drove in second till we came in sight of Johnny's car. It
faced us and we stopped. Max got out, leaving the machine
running, walked slowly to Johnny's car, and circled it.

He touched nothing, but that didn't mean that anything, no matter how immaterial and unrelated to murder, escaped his scrutiny. I am sure that Max could have
drawn a picture of Johnny's custom-built job complete
with any scratches that might be on the fenders and the
cigarette burn on the upholstery. He strolled back to his
own car, giving the ground the same careful raking from
side to side with his eyes.

"Someone was parked facing us," he gestured. "Right in front of Johnny. Johnny must have driven up behind and stopped when he found this car. I hardly think it was Bill's; bigger."

Relief made me lightheaded. I said, "Don't tell me you don't know the make?" I stopped trembling.

Max gave me a quick look. "You're being sarcastic. I was talking to myself, and the make doesn't matter. The wheel base is longer, the tire marks larger. Bill's car is a Ford, right?" I nodded. Max's look traveled out over the distance to the far hills. He had been talking to himself. He put his tongue in his cheek, his mind darting away, selecting, rejecting, classifying. I opened my mouth several times to speak, thought better of the idea, and kept silent.

Max drew a deep breath finally, expelled it, and said, "I can't remember his tires, but these are definitely money jobs. Big Buick, might be custom built. Or an Oldsmobile or a Lincoln Zephyr." Max brought his glance back to the path that led to the house. "He drove away by circling the drive and back, right past Johnny and going very, very fast."

Max moved toward his car. He shook his head. "Must have been in one hell of a hurry."

I grabbed at the straw, feeling weak. "Then you think it couldn't have been Bill! You'll——"

"Abbie," he said, "don't heckle me! I'm having nothing to do with this, thank you. That part of my life is over and done with, praise God! Never again do I want to hunt— that way."

He climbed in, swung the car to the left, clearing Johnny's by an unnecessarily large margin, and we careened down the path with our right wheels in the center between the ruts and our left well off the road and in the ditch.

I hung onto the side of the car desperately. "It'll do no good to be careful of tire tracks now, Max. We've already gone over them."

"I'm just not adding insult to injury."

In ten minutes we were at Old Village. We turned into the main street. Max swung to the curb and, braking swiftly, honked. There was a police car approaching slowly. It stopped, and at Max's gesture an officer got out and crossed the road.

Max said, "Hello." He hooked his elbow over the open window and leaned forward. "Don't think I know you, do I? We're on our way to the town hall and Chief Ingram, but I guess you'll do."

The officer shook his head and said, "I'm Fogarty."

"My name is Johnson."

He was a personable young man, fresh-faced and wholesome looking, with muscles that bulged under his dark blue shirt. He put a foot on the running board and said, "What can I do for you?"

"We've found a dead man and we think it's murder."

The young man snatched his foot back as if the car were hot. He made a whistling sound. "Where?"

"Up on Marrowback. At Miss Harris' place." Max thumbed in my general direction.

Fogarty said, "Hold everything till I get the chief."

He crossed the road abruptly, and we could hear the peculiarly harsh and hollow sound of the two-way radio. "Let me have the chief. Yes—Fogarty. Guy here says there is a dead body in a house on Marrowback. . . . Find out how you get there?"

Fogarty broke off to holler across the road, "How do you get there?"

Max opened the door, got out, and crossed to the police car. He gave directions, and Fogarty relayed them. I could hear the man at the other end say, "Get up there, Fogarty; you know what to do. I'll be there in ten minutes."

Max came back to the car, backed it into a driveway, turned around, and we retraced our steps to the Dead End sign. There Max stopped and went back to explain to Fogarty about the car, Johnny's car.

We drove on into the gloom of the tree-shaded climb, keeping between the ruts and well off the road. We stopped before we reached Johnny's car, and Fogarty got his chief on the radio again. He explained about the one track. We walked, rather quickly, up to the house.

Nothing had changed, except that the sun was a little higher, the house a little hotter. Fogarty got out a notebook and led the way. Max and I followed him as far as the door between the kitchen and the living room, in a silence that was dread and complete. Fogarty stepped inside, looked around, and turned back to us. I began my silly trembling again and sank to a kitchen chair. I wondered if Fogarty had ever seen a dead body before; he looked so young, so like an apple-cheeked farm boy.

He said, a little nervously, I thought, "Well, there is just so much to get done, and I might as well get started." He flipped back the cover of his book, took a pencil out of his pocket, and wrote, doing his thinking aloud.

"Time—eleven, exactly, July third, nineteen hundred and forty-six." He looked at me. "Your name, please." I told him, and Max repeated his.

"You aren't supposed to talk to each other," Fogarty

said, "but I guess you've had plenty of time to do that. That rule must mean witnesses who haven't met."

Max and I agreed. Five minutes passed. We went out onto the porch and looked down the drive. Fogarty followed us.

"Did you see—see it done? Oh no. I remember now. You said you found the body." He seemed a little depressed. Another five minutes passed and he brightened. "Well! Here comes the chief."

Striding purposefully and swiftly toward us from the gloom of the shaded track came a slender man in the dark blue shirt and trousers that was the summer uniform of Old Village's police. He pushed his visored cap back on his head as he reached the last steep slope to the house. Fogarty leaped from the porch to meet him as a wolf cub greets his food-foraging progenitor. I half expected him to fawn.

"Hi, Chief."

"Fogarty! Hello, Johnson." He held out a hand to Max. Max pumped his arm furiously. "Ingram! Still beating your brains out in Old Village!"

Ingram nodded, smiling widely, black eyes snapping with pleasure. I looked at him curiously. I had seen him at a distance often, but had never gotten to meet the man. I knew he had gone to school with Max, met a girl here at Ogg Lake one summer and married her, to settle down in Old Village. I saw a handsome man, whiplike and wiry, with a mouthful of white teeth and hair that was graying at the temples.

He said to Max, "Been matching any pennies lately?"

Max stuck out his lower lip and shook his head. "Remember that bird with the bald head and the fuzzy sideburns?"

Ingram laughed aloud. "He was a tough guy to shave, wasn't he? I still think he had a nickel with two heads."

Fogarty coughed. Max remembered me finally and introduced me. "Ingram and I," he explained, "went to school together. We used to work that train out of Buffalo—matching pennies." The two old college classmates exchanged another reminiscent look. "Made our fare, too, every time except that once."

Ingram said, "And you had to call your dad!"

Fogarty coughed again.

Ingram drew a deep breath, putting the dim past behind him. "Well! Where do we stand?"

Fogarty told him, looking to Max for help occasionally. Ingram held out his hand for the notes Fogarty had taken. He spoke decisively. "Get back to the car and call the sheriff—make the usual courtesy call. Then get the station and ask for three officers—Disbrow, Wentis, and Etter. Disbrow will be home in bed, but they'll dig him out. Get them up here."

"You go down to the turnoff to this road and stop anyone from driving up—we may want to work on those tracks. Make them walk."

Fogarty groaned. Ingram relented. "O.K. Just see that they follow our tracks and keep off the others. You better not turn your car around; back it down the road. Put a call through to the coroner and start the ball rolling with the photographer. Take those guys an hour to get here."

Fogarty left. We followed Ingram up onto the porch. He turned and called to the retreating officer, "Bring me the kit—you know—before you do anything else." Not waiting for an answer, he swung into the house. Max and I trotted behind him. I wished I had stayed in the car.

Then again, he might not have allowed me; I found the same kitchen chair and resumed my shaking.

Fogarty appeared in a moment, carrying a small suitcase. Max took it from him and, placing it on the kitchen table, flipped the clasps and opened it. Fogarty disappeared.

Ingram said, "Thanks. You know what I want, don't you, Johnson?"

I stretched my neck and peeked inside the case. It contained a conglomeration of odd, unrelated things. A small handsaw, a hammer, and a steel tape. A compass and a flashlight. A large tablet of plain paper and a like tablet of graph paper. A peculiar apparatus that looked like a hospital job, all glass tubing with rubber connections. Blotting paper and assorted sizes of pillboxes. Small glass bottles, several sheets of tissue paper, and a packet of cellophane bags.

Ingram said, "It'll be a while before the boys get here. Want to get a tissue and a bag, Johnson? We'll look around for the cartridge case. You see it?" He moved into the living room, took in the disorder with one quick glance, and paid it the tribute of a sharp and surprised whistle.

Max said, "Nope," and joined Ingram. The two of them stood in the middle of the room and did a careful and silent survey.

Ingram pointed to Johnny and finally said, "He was hit hard enough to throw him up against the wall. What do you bet it was an army forty-five automatic?"

Max said, "They'll be floating around for years. Any killings in the next ten years will be done with those babies."

Ingram nodded. "And half the accidents." He backed

up nearer the cots. "By the direction—by the hole in the wall—I'd say he stood here." He stretched his right arm and sighted along the pencil he held. At Max's nod he patted the top of the cot nearest him. "Case would throw right."

Max stepped over and drew the cover of the other cot taut. Nothing. Ingram dropped to his knees and peered under his cot. Reaching with his pencil, he rolled a small copper object out to the light. Carefully he inserted the point of the pencil in the hollow tube and lifted it up to deposit it in the piece of tissue Max held ready. They both stood up, drew together, and scrutinized it thoughtfully, as if it could tell them something. Max dropped it, finally, in the cellophane bag that Ingram, in his turn, held. He folded the top over and put it into his breast pocket.

Max said, "At first I looked for a rifle hole." He indicated the window.

"Forty-five, all right." Ingram shook his head.

I said, "Here come your boys, Mr. Ingram." My teeth chattered like a loose window in a high wind.

"Thanks." He walked through the kitchen and out onto the porch to greet them. "Hello, boys. Sorry to get you up, Disbrow."

"That's O.K., Chief."

"You take the door, Wentis. Not likely that anyone will come up here, unless the newspaper boys find us. But you stay on the porch anyway."

"Right," said Wentis, and sat down on the steps. He took out a pack of cigarettes. When his cigarette was lighted he stood up, walked carefully, respectfully into the living room, looked around, and went back to resume his seat on the steps.

Ingram said, "Etter, you get the steel tape, and you, Disbrow, the old graph paper. We'll get this over with."

The two young men did as they were told. They set to work in the big room with all the appearance of doing routine work. Again I wondered how many murders these boys handled in the course of a year.

They began at the left and, moving clockwise, measured every object in the room with relation to every other object. Disbrow laid a large sheet of graph paper on the floor and, getting down on his knees, filled everything in to scale as Etter called off the measurements.

Max and Ingram talked. I began to wonder what Maggie must be thinking. I half expected Mommie to arrive in search of her husband. But then she might think he had gone almost anywhere to sketch.

Once Ingram walked out to me and said, "I'm not just ignoring you, Miss Harris. The time for questioning you will be when we get to the station. Right now I want to get a picture of the crime. And," he added, "you'd be surprised how little time I have to do just that."

I said, "Yes, I suppose so," supposing nothing of the sort and clasping my hands in a desperate effort to stop shaking.

He explained. "When this gets around we'll be overrun with people, and all of them official."

Max followed Ingram. He said, "I want to see you get the bullet out of that wall."

"Didn't go through?" Ingram spun to stare at the wall.

"No, I looked. See?"

Ingram turned to the suitcase on the kitchen table and picked up the hammer. He looked around.

I said, "What?"

"Newspaper?"

I jumped up, glad to find something to do. There were no newspapers. He settled for an old piece of brown wrapping paper I found in the storeroom.

He spread it next to the wall on the kitchen side of the wall against which Johnny lay. He tapped experimentally, left off long enough to step around and measure the height of the bullet hole, then begin to chip away the plaster. He came upon the bullet almost immediately. Max held another piece of tissue while Ingram carefully flicked the small lead object out of the wall with the corner of his handkerchief wrapped around his first finger. Max put it into another cellophane bag, and Ingram deposited it in the same breast pocket with the cartridge case.

Ingram said to me, "What's in the room where you found the paper?"

I picked up the paper of plaster dust and took it with me as I showed Ingram. I dropped it into the nearest corner of what was the first of two bedrooms, now empty except for the junk Bill and Johnny had discarded. An old washstand, some crockery that they had not felt the need to use, a backless rocker, some empty bushel baskets, and a pile of magazines. On top of the magazines lay some more wrapping papers. Ingram unfolded these and read the addresses.

He said, "Where do they throw their junk?"

I said, "Out back, probably. They haven't been here long enough to have thrown out much."

We returned to the kitchen, and I showed Ingram the back door. He walked around in the yard, kicking over a basket and giving the contents a casual scrutiny, even going as far as the little house, stepping high to clear the weeds. He came back to the doorway and spent the next ten minutes picking off burdocks, cussing good-naturedly.

FIVE

I went out onto the porch and sat down beside the officer there. There was no friendliness in the atmosphere. Wentis wasn't inclined to talk; his face was an interesting study in controlled curiosity. I respected his silence, but I kept my seat, sinking my chin in the palms of both hands, elbows on my knees. Suppose I had done the awful deed? I could almost see his mind lining up his thoughts, building a good story to entertain his wife with at dinner. He began to chew his gum a little faster.

There was a bellow from the depths of the tree-shaded lane, and I jumped, brought both knees up sharply, biting my tongue. Wentis paled and lost the rhythm of his jaw movement. I had known Dr. Custom would arrive sooner or later, but I had thought he would save his breath for the climb from the car to the house. A steep climb would be against his wishes, and I knew that he, without a doubt, had put up a nice struggle when the officer in charge had said, "Here's where you get off and walk, Doctor." I got up and went to meet him.

Dr. Fitzgerald Custom is one of the oldest friends I have. I might have married him long ago if he had been six inches taller than his five feet four and weighed a little less than his one hundred and eighty.

I said, "Hello, Doctor."

He didn't hear me, but he began laughing for no reason that I could see. He has a jolly disposition, with a booming laugh that can be started more easily than it can be stopped. His eyes are black and alert and knowing under heavy black brows, and his hair is thick and wavy and white. He is a handsome man, a little on the finicky-fastidious, always smelling nice, inclined to be faddish in his habits. He smoked nothing but denicotinized cigarettes, drank nothing but decaffeinized coffee with his meals, and yet he'd overeat at the drop of the hat and I never yet have heard him order a de-alcoholized cocktail. I like the man. I widened my nostrils now, as I drew near him, anticipating that clean, doctor-office odor combined with the immaculate male grooming that is Dr. Custom.

He was waving his short arms about like the propellers on a bimotor plane, shouting to the world in general and to no one in particular, "I knew it, I knew it, I knew it! I saw Johnson's car and I said to myself, 'Alberta Harris! She's done it again.'" The doctor's jokes weren't always in good taste.

"Hush," I said. "You're getting too close for comfort."

Dr. Custom put his arm around me and we climbed the path side by side, the little man huffing and puffing like a steam engine up the side of a mountain. Max and Troy Ingram heard him and came out of the house to watch us from the porch. The young officer, Wentis, stood up and ceased chewing gum altogether for the moment. I stopped abruptly at the steps, and the doctor bounded up onto the porch to shake hands with the three men with all the enthusiasm of a late arrival at a social event.

They went inside. That left me alone with Wentis once more. He avoided my eyes self-consciously and resumed his ruminative chewing, studiously examining the weathered old barn in the immediate foreground and then the hills in the blue distance. . . . I probably had done it! Without a doubt I had done it! And with such a strong ally as Dr. Custom, the county coroner, they'd never pin it on me!

Max and Ingram and Dr. Custom came out presently.

Dr. Custom said, "Say, my lad, run down to my car and bring me the blanks. You'll find them in the glove compartment or on the back window—look around. Forgot them."

Wentis jerked his eyes away from the barn. "Blanks?"

"Blanks, boy, blanks. How do you think we're going to get this lad officially dead without blanks to fill out?" Dr. Custom produced a cigarette case and offered me a denicotinized cigarette, which I refused. He lighted one for himself with his lighter and made an impatient gesture in the direction of the trees. "Window ledge—back window ledge." Wentis departed rather quickly.

Ingram said, "Before midnight, you say?"

"Absolutely. One shot straight through the heart and zingo——"

The gum-chewing Wentis made the return trip from Dr. Custom's car at a dogtrot, keeping time with his jaws, and handed over the papers. Immediately behind him came a tall individual with flapping ears, sloping narrow shoulders, and bulging pockets. He trotted as a pendulum swings, from side to side, in one hand a camera complete with flash bulb and in the other a box.

After greeting each other they went inside the house, leaving me to the silent and suspicious company of Wentis. There were small booms and bright blue flashes coming from the house in the next half hour. I felt a headache threatening.

Presently the six men trooped out. They set their various cases of official paraphernalia down on the porch, seeming in no hurry to get on about their businesses. The morgue wagon dashed up the slope with a powerful, silent speed and an officer hanging on the running board importantly.

He dropped off before the vehicle stopped, explaining with a happy smile, "I rode along, Chief; didn't trust these city slickers not to ride in the tracks."

My headache became more than a threat; it was a grim reality. I decided that unless the murderer or murderee was a member of your immediate family, investigating the crime was an exceedingly exciting pastime. And fairly safe for most of the boys. They didn't appear to be the least bit moved by the finality, the sadness, the infinitude of sudden death. Head averted and stomach sick, I hurried down the path and climbed into Max's car. No one noticed or objected. I closed my eyes.

In a short while I heard the morgue wagon tear past me. I didn't open my eyes to see if Ingram's man took the return trip on the running board. I leaned my head up against the side of the car and pressed my hands to my temples. They were throbbing and thumping like a bass drum when struck by an enthusiastic and rhythmic drummer.

Another half hour passed. Dr. Custom left. He stopped long enough to say with a leer, "Do you want me to make Ingram let you go, or are you willing to take your medicine like a man?" I favored him with a glare. Hadn't the man any finer sensibilities? Or had I neglected to tell him how this murder struck close to home and how I would never believe that lightning couldn't strike twice? I decided against a bid for sympathy and left it with a glare. And I forgot to mention the headache, but if the man had a heart in his body he could see I was suffering, couldn't he?

Max and Ingram covered both incoming and outgoing tracks. Covered them thoroughly and discussed them, to my mind, unnecessarily long. It was cool under the trees.

I deliberately made my mind a blank and had almost dozed off when Max climbed under the wheel of the car. I sat up straight and said, "What now?"

"Now? We go to Ingram's office and tell all."

Ingram's office consisted of a partitioned-off space in the half of the Old Village town hall that was devoted to law enforcement. I sat at the side of his desk in a chair that looked uncomfortable but wasn't, and Ingram, face pleasantly expressionless, asked questions while another young man in uniform took notes at a desk set at right angles to us. I wondered just how many young men Ingram had at his beck and call. So far I had counted six.

What could I tell him about the deceased?

I pressed my temples once more with my fingers, trying desperately to assemble my thoughts in some sort of order. My throat still hurt and I was thirsty. The man, Ingram, was so swift in his manner, so sure of himself, so obviously but not objectionably master of the situation, I couldn't help feeling clumsy. I took my hands down from my head and clasped them in my lap.

Watch yourself, Abbie. Talk all you wish about Johnny, but forget you have a nephew—don't mention Bill. Don't say he is not responsible for all his actions—don't say he should be in a hospital—kept quiet—watched.

I cleared my throat. "John Rutland—age thirty—ex-flier from the Pacific area—friend of my nephew—professional painter—some independent means—I couldn't say how much or from what source."

"Married?"

"My nephew says so, but I have never discussed it with John Rutland."

"Did the nephew say where the wife is?"

"No."

"Where does he hail from—where are his people?" Ingram smiled a little and explained, "John Rutland, not your nephew."

"I understand he has none."

"Where's his home?"

"I don't have the faintest idea." I began to feel that perhaps Maggie and I were not quite bright to have harbored a man about whom we knew so little. I tried to look intelligent.

"What was he doing here?" Ingram wasn't impatient—in fact, I came to realize that he was the most patient of men—but he was so naturally quick, cutting his words off sharply and clearly, forming another question as you were answering the first one, that I had the sensation of avoiding his questions. Especially as some of the answers sounded evasive even as I spoke.

I said, "I told you, Mr. Ingram, that my nephew, Bill, invited him to spend the summer here. They were to paint."

"Just the two of them?"

"Just the two of them."

Ingram tore off a page of his scratch pad, crumpled it into a ball, and dropped it into the basket beside his desk. He began on another. "Tell me what your nephew was doing here. His name."

I told him Bill's name and explained how he had surprised us.

He said, "How did your nephew get Rutland to come here? Write?"

"No," I said. "He phoned, long-distance."

Ingram made a satisfied sound. He left off making marks on the pad before him and swiveling in his chair; he called

to yet another man in a dark blue uniform. That made
seven. "Russell."

Russell appeared at the door. "Yes, sir."

"Get down to the telephone office, find out where a
long-distance call went that was charged to——" He raised
his brows at me inquiringly.

I said, "It's listed under Papa's name—we've neglected
to change it. William Henry Harris, Harris Cove, Ogg
Lake."

Ingram wrote it down, looked at me again, and asked,
"Date?"

I fumbled around in my poor, aching head once more
and produced Monday, June twenty-fourth. I hoped, fer-
vently, that I was right. Ingram seemed satisfied. He
handed the slip of paper to Russell, who departed. Ingram
turned again to me. He chewed his underlip thoughtfully
and inspected me with his black eyes as if he could read
from my facial expression the place where he had left off
his questioning.

The stenographer at the other desk prompted him.
"'How did your nephew get Rutland to come here?
Write?' Answer: 'No. He phoned, long-distance.'"

Ingram said, "Thanks!" and continued to stare at me. I
stared back. He spoke finally, tapping his scratch pad
with the eraser end of the pencil. "Most of these things
are fairly simple—you can sum it up in one word: sex."

I didn't reply. He hadn't meant me to, though I could
have argued that, to my mind, sex is never simple. It is anything else but.

There was a rustle out in the main room. I could feel
something important about to happen; chairs scraped,
people stood, and those who didn't stand at least
straightened up in their seats.

Ingram pushed his chair back, stood, and, walking around me, opened the connecting door. He said, and there was respect in his voice, "Hi, Young. Had your lunch?"

"Not yet." They shook hands. "How are you, Ingram?"

"Can't complain." Ingram stepped aside, gesturing the man into the office. The man matched his voice; nothing but a barrel body could have produced those resonant chest tones. A big man, slow in his movements, deliberate, decisive, with a commanding carriage, chin up, eyes calm, body balanced easily on the balls of his feet. He smiled at me. I rose to my feet and smiled back.

Ingram introduced us. "Have you met our district attorney, Miss Harris? No? This is Mr. Clarence Young, Miss Harris. Miss Alberta Harris, Mr. Young."

I said, "How do you do."

He said, "How do you do."

I sat, and he lowered himself into the chair Ingram had vacated. Ingram handed him the data Etter and Disbrow had collected at the house, together with his own notes and the two cellophane envelopes containing the bullet and the cartridge case. Young studied them, asking Ingram pointed and intelligent questions. At last he leaned back in his chair. I could see that he had a picture of events to date.

At this point a man with an apron around his middle arrived with a covered tray of food and a note from Dr. Custom. Clipped to the note was a powder in a folded paper. The note read: "Take powder with glass of water—it'll fix your head. I knew where you'd be for the next two hours, so I stopped at the lunch wagon and had them fix some food for you. Now, give Max his share, you pig. Tried to call Maggie but that nine-party line of your——

Be good and tell all. Nothing but biology keeps me from your side."

Bless the man! And how had he known I had this head? A warm glow filled the place that had harbored the knotty lump inside me. I swallowed the powder with a glass of water obediently, drawing a golden halo above the mental picture I carried of my favorite doctor.

I lifted the napkins and found that I was ravenous. Ingram gave me permission to go out into the general room, and I shared the food with Max. Ingram sent a couple of officers out for his and the district attorney's lunches.

After we had eaten, Young said, "Well! I think I have the situation, Ingram. I'll carry on for a while, but"—he looked at his watch—"I want to get up to that place before dark."

I went back to my chair beside the desk, refreshed and minus the headache. Ingram brought in another chair from the outer room. He said to the district attorney, "I haven't gone through the fellow's things yet. I'll wait and do it when you go up to look around."

"Good!" He turned to me. "Now, Miss Harris. Did this young man have any enemies? Do you know?"

The man Russell appeared from nowhere and handed Ingram a slip of paper.

"No," I said, "but I hadn't known him quite a week."

"I want you to give me a list of the people you know who knew him." He held out a large white hand and accepted the slip of paper from Ingram. He read it, looked up quickly, and said, "What does it mean—Woodstock, New York?"

Ingram explained, "Forgot to tell you, Young; you weren't here. Woodstock"—he tapped the paper with a brown finger—"where Rutland was living before he came here. Miss Harris' nephew, Bill Hunt, called him there on that date, June twenty-fourth."

Young considered it. He laid the paper on the sheaf of data already before him and repeated his question. "Give me a list of the people you know who knew him."

It wasn't a long list. "My sister Maggie, my nephew Bill, Max and Mommie Johnson, Mommie's father, and Virginia Lane." I felt as though I should apologize.

Young tipped his big head on one side and put his elbow on one knee, bringing an enormous fist under my nose. He uncurled his fingers at me, and I could see the polish on his manicured nails. It was colorless. "Do you mean to say that in a week at Ogg Lake a young man of thirty got to know—let me see—six people?" He fanned his fingers and added the first finger of the other hand to make six. He leaned back and brought his hands down against his knees. "My, but he led a restricted life!"

I wasn't so sure I was going to like Mr. Clarence Young. He held distinctly nasty possibilities under that suave exterior. But I stood my ground. "I didn't tag along with him wherever he went." I said it stiffly, trying to look as distant as possible. "He may have met people down at the Point, and then there was that blonde in the car with the Texas license."

"Now we're getting somewhere!" He tipped his chair, hooking his arm over the back, clasping a knee with his free hand, and favoring me with a satisfied smile. This was going to be easy! Sex was simple! "What blonde? In what Texas car?"

I told him the little I knew about her, which added up to exactly nothing, feeling my heart go sick again at the memory of Bill's white-lipped, pain-drawn face.

The man read my expression. He snapped his chair to the floor, brought his arm down, and placed both hands on his knees. He tapped his fingers impatiently. "Come now, Miss Harris! You aren't breathing hard at the memory of a blonde about whom you know nothing!"

I said, "I'm sorry." I clamped my jaws in what I fancied was a firm manner and tried to make my breathing normal.

Clarence Young bestowed upon me a soft, melting, blue-eyed invitation to confide in him. A sweet, professional, good-natured smile that made a lie out of the sharpness of his "Come now." A clock on the wall clicked electrically, jumping a three-minute interval. He continued to regard me pleasantly, tipping his head again, straining the elastic of our mutual affability to the thinness of a hair. I remained silent, wanting to blink my eyes against the blue light from his.

He spoke finally, very softly. "What's your nephew's name?"

I told him.

He said, "Where did you say he's from?"

I hadn't said, but I named the suburb of Chicago and the state of Illinois.

"And this lad who was shot?" The blue eyes never winked, never lost that genial, ingratiating glow.

Affability became no longer mutual. On my end it snapped. I said, "I hadn't said; it was Mr. Ingram. Woodstock, New York."

"Woodstock, New York," he repeated. He made a sucking noise. "I see." Clarence Young appeared to lose interest in me. His chair creaked a little as he swiveled to the desk and touched the pile of data Ingram had there, patting it affectionately.

The door opened to admit an officer. One I had seen before, so that left my count at seven. He laid a piece of paper before Ingram and departed, after stating that he had done nothing about this until Ingram became a little less busy, but now Mr. Young mentioned Illinois he thought Ingram would be interested. He was.

Ingram said, "Thanks," and read the message.

Clarence Young spun around and faced me once more. He said, "Where did you say the blonde was from?"

"Texas," I answered.

Ingram reached out with a slender, muscular hand and touched Clarence Young's sleeve. The district attorney turned with raised eyebrows. Ingram addressed me. "Your nephew from Illinois?"

I nodded.

Ingram consulted the paper again, raised black eyes to mine. "Does he drive a car, and what kind?"

My heart pounded uncomfortably. I said, "A blue convertible. Ford."

"Year?"

I shook my head. I couldn't say; they all look alike to me. Max called out from the other room, "A 'forty-one."

Ingram said, "Thanks." To Clarence Young he explained, "A call came through while we were out this morning reporting a 'forty-one Ford convertible with an Illinois license abandoned south of here. Town Line Road near the inlet to Ogg Lake. Farmer called."

The district attorney looked very happy. I could have slapped him. He said, loud and jolly, "Sounds like his! Eh, Miss Harris?"

I nodded dumbly.

He lowered his voice, dismissing me. "That'll be all for now. Thank you." He stood courteously and held the door for me.

Max went in, making a circle of the thumb and first finger of his right hand and snapping the gesture in my direction. It should have made me feel better. It didn't.

Ingram passed into the back room, returned, and gave Clarence Young a bundle. I heard him say, "This is the contents of the glove compartment of his car. Nail file, road maps, New York State driver's license, car registration, and some letters from an Iris Martin Rutland, 166 Main Street, Royal, Texas. Shall I telegraph the usual to Royal?"

Clarence Young said, "Hmm, Texas. You can let it ride a bit. I've an idea she's closer than that." He turned to Max and began on him where he had left off with me. The blonde.

Max said, "I haven't met the woman."

"But you've heard about her," Clarence Young insisted.

"Yes."

"When?"

"Yesterday."

"Where were you yesterday?"

"At Blue Horizon."

"And who—I take it Blue Horizon is the artistic name of the place where the man John Rutland was killed—and who told you about the blonde?"

Max explained. Clarence Young interrupted. "Do you mean to tell me that a blonde looking for——" He consulted Ingram.

Ingram supplied the name for him.

"—looking for William Hunt, Miss Harris' nephew, came to call on—what's the name—John Rutland?"

I could imagine Max spreading his hands in that familiar gesture that meant, "I know you won't believe me—but it's true."

The district attorney came to the door of the office and beckoned with a toss of his head. He said, "Come back in here, please, Miss Harris."

I obeyed. The men stood politely. I refused the chair Max offered. I looked at Clarence Young.

"Where is your nephew?" he asked.

I said wearily, "I don't know."

"Didn't I understand you to say that he was living for the summer with this—let me see—John Rutland at the place called Blue Horizon?"

"Yes."

"Did I understand you to say he was very fond of—your nephew was very fond of John Rutland?"

"He was his best friend."

"Where did they meet? How did they know each other?"

"In the Pacific, I think."

"Don't you know?"

"No."

"How did they get along?"

I lifted my shoulder and remained silent.

After a pause wherein Clarence Young managed to suggest patience, he said, "Have you ever seen them quarrel?"

I didn't answer. I felt miserable. My face must have mirrored the contraction of my heart, for the district attorney made a satisfied sound.

He answered his own query. "They had a fight?"

I kept my lips together and tried not to blink. He insisted.

"Yesterday?"

I was dumb. I felt tears sting my eyes.

Clarence Young sighed. "Ah! Now we're getting places. Where would your nephew head for? Where'll we start looking?"

As if I'd say if I did know! I felt the tears dry with the heat of the flush that suffused my face. I stared with as much insolence as I could muster at the smooth, pale face above me. The saucer blue eyes stared back at me happily, like a cat at a fish in a bowl.

Clarence Young looked at his watch. He spoke decisively. "He won't get far without his car. Get going on that, Ingram. Then let's you and me take a look at that house. Two o'clock. Can I have a couple of your men bring in the people Miss Harris so kindly gave me a list of?"

Ingram made a gesture to the secretary, who scribbled off a list and handed it to him.

Clarence Young said, "Thank you. Let's go."

Max stopped Ingram as he was going through the door. "You can depend on me to bring in my wife, Ingram; just name the time."

Ingram smiled. "What time shall I say, Young?"

Clarence was at the outer door. He called back, "What time for what?"

"What time do you want to do the rest of the questioning?"

"Say four or five."

"Right." Ingram nodded to Max.

Max said, "I'd like to be responsible for Maggie Harris and Bill Hunt if I find him. My father-in-law won't be home from the office till after six."

Ingram said, "You know it ain't legal—but you go ahead, Johnson. I know when I'm lucky. I'll be down to the cove later to take care of the neighbors."

Max and I arrived home at two-fifteen. Mommie hailed us from the end of the dock, where she was sunning herself. It was apparent that she expected Max to join her, and he did. There was no sign of the children. The baby must be in bed napping; the other girls, no doubt, were on the lake somewhere, probably swimming.

I found Maggie on the glider on the porch. "Well," she said, "where have you been?"

"Don't say a word to me," I said. "I'm exhausted. I'll tell you about it in a minute."

Maggie took me literally and sank back against the cushions on the glider and waited patiently.

I said, "Haven't had a call from Bill, have you?"

"He's sound asleep."

"Asleep!" I jumped to my feet, knocking the rocker against the side of the house with a crash.

Maggie sat up straight. "Abbie. Have you taken leave?"

I resisted the impulse to race up the stairs and verify; I sank slowly to the rocker again. I said, "Who's been using the line? We've been trying to get you for hours."

"Not I. Bill must have come in in the night. I was about to ask you if you hadn't heard him. And where is his car?"

I told her where his car was and the events leading to my knowledge of the whereabouts. Maggie heard me out wordlessly, got up and went to the kitchen, where I could hear her making a pot of tea. Maggie's antidote for anything, be it pleasant or unpleasant, is tea. Maggie has something there.

SIX

I moved over to the glider when Maggie handed me a cup of hot strong tea. The cup rattled against the saucer as I took it.

Maggie pulled up a rocker and said, "Now give it to me again and slower."

I repeated the morning's events between unladylike gulps of steaming liquid. I answered questions, and with one ear I listened for the sounds of a nephew getting up. Maggie read my mind.

"I'll wake him in a minute. First I want——" She left the porch, and I heard her in the utility and furnace room that we use for storage, then in Papa's study. What could she possibly want with the heirloom glass stored in the cabinet there?

Presently she appeared carrying a tray on which stood an urn-shaped bottle of Croizet and four small glasses. My mouth dropped open. That brandy must be at least one hundred and twenty years old—the last of what Papa called his wake-and-wedding welcome—and those small glasses date back to Napoleon.

"Maggie," I gasped, "we aren't—— This is no time—— You can't celebrate!"

"I'm not trying to celebrate." Maggie's placid manner remained unruffled. "We aren't—and this is the time, I figure, for something stronger than tea; call it medicine. Now stop sputtering."

Maggie had a little trouble with the cork. It broke and she finally shoved it down into the bottle, dust and all.

As if we had signaled, Mommie and Max strolled in from their dock, crossed the lawns, and entered the porch by the side door.

Upstairs a shower was turned on.

Mommie curled up on the other end of the glider and accepted her drink. She tasted it, looked up quickly and appreciatively at Maggie, and, with a surprised sound, snuggled down happily, both hands on the tiny glass.

Maggie spoke aggressively to no one in particular. "Bill didn't."

Max said nothing and departed kitchenward. We heard the icebox door open and close. He emerged, a bottle of beer in one hand, a glass in the other, to station himself against a post in that familiar position, one shoulder higher than the other, one lean leg crossed over its mate. He poured his beer, carefully tipping the glass to the bottle so as to avoid a collar.

Maggie repeated, "Bill did not do it! It's silly for Ingram —— Why, I like the boy—love him."

I said, for no particular reason except to twist the knife of memory, "I liked the other Bill."

Mommie, her blue eyes oversized and serious under her peaked black brows, said, "I didn't, and I do, this Bill."

Max held his glass up to the light. "I'll feel better after I talk to the guy. Where the heck——" He drank.

"And I'm dread——" I said. "Maggie, you don't think this family carries some kind of taint?"

Upstairs the shower turned off.

Maggie lifted the brandy bottle gently and slowly filled our glasses again. Mommie purred. Max wrinkled his nose distastefully. Maggie looked a little unsure of herself, a little frightened, but her soft voice was firm. "We've traveled a long way from Bible times, and the sins-of-the-father stuff can all be explained psychologically." She replaced the bottle and pressed her hands down on the table as if to steady herself.

Max heard the shower and interpreted it. He gave me an inquiring look and I nodded. He uncrossed his long legs. Mommie said, "I almost popped a pantie button."

There was a sound from the living room. Bill stood in the doorway. "Why, how you talk, Mrs. Johnson." He took two long strides to the table and examined the bottle of brandy. "My gosh!" He shook his head. "It's too early and too hot to lap that stuff up."

We stared as one and regarded the Harris nephew.

He looked a little like the breaking up of a hard winter in a young, red-eyed, freshly-showered-and-shaved way. His hair lay wet and wavy on his head and there were dark shadows under the brown eyes. He backed up and leaned against the doorjamb with his hands thrust into his pockets as though he didn't trust himself to stand alone.

Maggie said, "Want some?"

"No, thank you. If there's a cold beer handy——" He crossed the porch and entered the kitchen. Again we heard the refrigerator door open and close and a beer cap tinkle to the sink. He was back in a moment.

"What's the matter with everyone? You look as if—— Say, Johnson, I ran out of gas last night. Had to walk home——" He broke off again and looked from one to the other of us, a puzzled wrinkle between his brows. "Will someone please let me in on things!"

I felt the sweat break out on the back of my knees. Bill dropped into the nearest rocker and placed his bottle on the sill of the window beside him.

Max sank to the floor, cross-legged, and put his bottle and glass between his feet. He said, "It's a dirty trick."

And immediately we all started to talk at once.

Mommie said, "To tell you like this——"

Maggie broke in with, "Believe me, we all like you, Bill——"

I said, "We hope you were playing poker all night——"

Bill laughed uncertainly and put his glass down beside the bottle on the sill. He held up both hands, protesting, "Well, I wasn't. For the love of Mike! Will someone please tell me what you're getting at?"

Max told him—brutally, bluntly, and in as few words as possible. The boy had the stuff. He got to his feet and paced, lips compressed, face white, but other than that he heard Max out without questions. When Max reached the end of the tale, Bill struck the palm of one hand with a fist and smiled shakily at Maggie and me.

"Tough on you two! I'm sorry, Aunts, I bothered you. And it seemed like such a good idea at the time, coming here!"

"Bill," said Maggie firmly, "where you belong is right here. What are families for if not to take care of their own?"

I said, "And we only worry about you."

Maggie said, "And you're not to worry about a thing. Max will take care of everything, won't you, Max?"

I held my breath.

Max did not hesitate. "You flatter me, Maggie." He poured the rest of the beer into his glass and motioned Bill back to his rocker.

Bill obeyed and picked up his beer. He drank deeply, set his glass back onto the sill, and hung his hands between his knees. He watched Max.

That gentleman took a sip of his beer. "Troy Ingram," he said, "is a smart lad, and this job is in his capable hands." He took a second sip. "Up until the time you stepped in that doorway," Max went on, "I thought I wanted nothing to do with this. Funny thing! As soon as I saw you I knew I'd tag along even if it——" He grinned a white, one-sided grin.

Maggie said, "What do we do first?"

Bill looked up. "What do you say we get my car? I think I could find it."

Max reached a hand under his shirt and scratched his middle thoughtfully. "I know where the car is. Yes—we'll do that first."

"But what are you going to do?" Maggie insisted.

Max raised his heavy brows and tipped his head. Maggie is usually the one who never hurries; now she was all in a dither. He said, "There is a set of rules. I learned them once, and I think I could recite them, if you wish."

Bill leaned forward in his chair and lowered his head into his hands and groaned. "Last night. I wish I could remember. I was looping, really looping, last night."

Maggie stuck to her idea. "What do you do first?"

"First," said Max, "comes 'Who?'. That we know. Then come the questions: friends, habits, enemies, and finances. Bill is our best bet for the answers."

Bill groaned again and sat up. "I am the only friend outside of the fellows in our outfit that I know of. Oh yes, I called him at a friend's house in Woodstock. I'd have to look up his name."

"Ingram is way ahead of you," said Max. "He has the name and probably will look up the friend, too."

"Enemies?" Bill asked himself. "I don't know of any. Habits? Average, I would say. Finances? Well, he didn't depend on his painting, though he was good. I never discussed money. He seemed to have enough."

Max said, "Apparent motive? Notice I said, 'Apparent.' In most murders the real and apparent motives are poles apart."

Bill was silent, head down in his hands once more. I said, "Apparently, either robbery or nasty, wanton destruction."

Bill raised his eyes. He and Maggie both looked puzzled. I explained the slitting of the paint tubes, the smearing of the walls and window.

Max shook his head. "Nope. We'll have to hunt for that. Who saw the victim last?"

No one spoke. Mommie asked for a cigarette. Bill jumped from his chair, was sorry an instant later when he staggered against the table. He said he was sorry, he had been looping, really looping, last night.

Max said, "Well, that'll come out."

I said, "Johnny went away somewhere, didn't he? Last night, I mean."

Max nodded. "Ingram will trace that. Not too hard. Next comes fixing the time. What did Doc Custom say, Abbie?"

"Before midnight," I told him.

Max said, "Next we should go back two weeks and find people who have visited the scene of the crime." He surveyed us, smiling.

We blinked. We hadn't been near the place in years, and Max knew it. Bill said, "Two weeks ago I was in Chicago and Johnny was in New York."

Max said, "Had enough? There are six more rules—want I should spare you? May take us many days to go through them."

The clock in the living room struck three. I said, "Spare us and get going. Remember your date with Ingram at four."

Max stood. "Right. Maggie, do you think you can bring Mommie up to the police station by four? Bill and I will meet you there."

Mommie said, "The baby?"

I said, "Silly! You know I'd love to."

Bill said, "I hope I can remember where I went last night." He picked up his and Max's bottles and deposited them in the case of empties in the utility room. He came back and rinsed out the glasses. They left.

I heard Max say, "You'd better."

Mommie got off the glider and called Max back. He came and stood outside the screen.

"What," she asked, "are Maggie and I to say about the exhibition the boys put on yesterday afternoon?"

"The truth, dopey. But nothing he doesn't ask for."

Mommie left, to get the baby dressed and change her own slack suit for a fresher one. I went upstairs and showered and changed my clothes. The bed looked tempting, but I resisted.

Maggie stuck her head around the door of her room. "I wonder if Bill has a gun?"

I did something I don't usually do. I did it without thinking, almost from a compulsion; I opened Bill's dresser drawers. Maggie stood over my shoulder, so she shares the shame. I didn't touch anything in the drawers; indeed there wasn't much there—just socks and shirts and shorts and a supply of handkerchiefs and sweaters. I didn't touch anything, because I didn't need to. The gun lay out in plain sight, and I didn't touch it. Maggie drew in her breath with a hiss and reached out a plump arm toward the snub-nosed instrument, thought better of it, and withdrew. I closed the drawer.

We made the bed in complete silence.

Maggie and Mommie didn't have to go to Old Village alone, after all. Max and Bill returned inside of forty-five minutes. So the four of them set out at four, leaving the baby and me, waving energetically, out by the mailboxes. As we walked back across the lawn I caught sight of the Lane cottage. I established the baby at her small, boat-filled pool with a thoughtful frown on my face.

Where were the Lanes? Virginia was usually out-of-doors and about. And Mrs. Lane can smell a drama a mile away! Where was she? And why hadn't one of us let Virginia know? Certainly she was an interested party! I had just plain forgotten.

I climbed the two steps to the Lane porch, pulled open the screen, and yoo-hooed.

Virginia came stumbling down the stairs, carrying a rubber bathing hat in one hand. She had on a yellow bathing suit that made her look like a brown-and-golden field flower. I told her so.

She didn't hear me. One look at her face told me that she wasn't having any news from me; she already knew. Her face was drained of all color, lips white, eyes enormous.

"Abbie!" She clutched the newel post, one bare foot pointed floorward. "There must be some mistake! The radio said—— I was getting into my suit just now—thought I might talk someone into a swim—— The radio said——"

I patted the white knuckles and tried to smile reassuringly. "Yes." The hand relaxed a little. I lifted a finger and bent it.

"But—why?"

"I don't know, dear."

"Why would anyone—— How awful, Abbie! How perfectly awful for you and Maggie and——"

I lifted the hand from the newel post. The girl stepped down.

A small face was flat-nosed against the screen. "I want to come in," demanded a high voice.

"Of course, honey." Slim brown legs carried Virginia to the door. She held the screen for the baby.

"Want a cooky?" Virginia asked.

The baby was already on a kitchen chair, straight little three-year-old legs together, fat little hands folded in anticipation. I followed her and sat in a chair on the other side of the table.

Virginia took a shuddering breath. She had to think before she replied. She laid her bathing cap on the table and lifted the cooky jar from the top of the refrigerator to the table.

"Oh, you know! Mother's guild and the annual picnic! She wanted me to go—it's every third of July—but I felt lousy."

The baby made an anticipatory noise, and Virginia gave her a cooky. I said, "I'm sorry." I helped myself to a cooky. Virginia took one.

I said, "Anything I can do?"

"Not unless you can advise me."

"Best thing I do, dear."

"I seem to be the kind of girl who is constantly getting into awkward situations and then . . ." Her voice trailed off. She looked at the cooky in her hand; it might well have been a paper job—obviously she didn't know it was edible. She began to crumble it on the oilcloth.

"What awkward situation?"

"Bill."

What did she mean? Did she mean she wished she hadn't known Bill now he was involved in Johnny's death? Or was it just plain Bill? I looked at the brown eyes across the table—frightened brown eyes. Open too wide, open too long. I blinked in sympathy.

The husky voice dropped to barely a whisper. "Remember the other Bill?"

As if I could ever forget! As if I could think of anyone else—had thought of anyone else in the last four or five hours! Was that boy to haunt the cove for all time?

Virginia pinched the cooky crumbs into a small pile.

She continued after a thick and longish pause wherein we both remembered the other Bill.

"Of course I was only nineteen at the time, but I was pretty crazy about the man—you know that. Then when it turned out so badly—I was afraid—of my own emotions. I still don't trust my own judgment."

"I know," I said. "We feel the same."

"In fact," Virginia explained, "this Bill—Bill Hunt— wrote to me for two years before I would let down—more than just the kind of letters you write to your old English teacher. And you know how easy it is to get to know a person by letter."

The baby scrambled down from her chair and went to the icebox. Virginia stretched out a hand, absently opened the door, and reached for the milk. The baby trotted over to the cupboard where the glasses were kept. Virginia got up and followed. She filled a glass too full and had to hold it while the baby drank. She gave me a half-smile over the curly head.

I said, "I do. I think anyone is inclined to reveal more in his letters than he will in, say, even a long acquaintance."

Virginia nodded her head up and down emphatically. She lifted the baby back to her chair and gave her another cooky. She went back to crumbling her own.

"The longer Bill wrote me, the better I liked him. And I mean like—not any silly, nineteen-year-old thinking-I'm-in-love stuff."

"I know what you mean," I said.

"Then we met again—and all of a sudden we were bashful with each other."

"Silly!" I smiled.

"Wasn't it? I guess we had told each other too much— about our innermost thoughts—our secret emotions—our

ambitions and our pet hates. There was no foundation of
—well, you know—doing the usual things—even touching
each other's hands."

"I know," I said. "But all that would follow naturally.
You knew the real Bill—the inside Bill, and—I still don't
know what you're getting at."

"He scares me and I scare him. I don't know what to do
about it."

"Darling, don't do anything! Just coast along and it will
all work out."

"I don't know. You saw what happened yesterday."

"Are you trying to tell me——"

Virginia leaned eagerly across the table, brushing her
hands together to clean them of crumbs. "Here's the way
I feel about it. If Bill couldn't see that what Johnny tried
to pull was none of my contriving—if he doesn't trust
me any more than——"

I made a small protesting gesture.

Virginia closed her eyes a moment. She made two fists
and rubbed them. "Violence scares me—after——"

"The other Bill?"

She nodded dumbly, lips compressed and trembling.
Color had come back into her face.

"Are you trying to say that you think Bill might have
a bad heritage—and you want none of it?"

"Something like that. Forgive me, Abbie."

"But, sweet, you don't have to——"

"But"—she spread her hands expressively—"I like him.
I hate to think I could be fooled——"

"Again?" I finished for her.

"Yes. I hate to think that I am no better judge of——
Oh, Abbie! I'm hurting your feelings, and I wouldn't for
the world."

"No," I said slowly. "My feelings aren't easily hurt. And I well know that in this selection business—love—or whatever you call it—it is the girl who does this—thinks of heritage—— Or should."

Virginia stood up impatiently. "I'm giving the impression that Bill and I—and we aren't—he hasn't——"

I smiled. "Stop fumbling, Virginia. I know what you want to say."

"Do you?" She sounded dubious and at the same time anxious that I should.

The baby slipped off her chair and made for the door. Virginia followed and spoke over one smooth shoulder. "I don't even like Johnny—I mean didn't—— In fact, I had trouble being nice to him. And I tried because he was a friend of Bill's."

We went out onto the porch, the baby racing to her small pool. Virginia went back into her house and returned with her cap. She got into the skiff, tied to her dock, and rowed out. She didn't swim, though, when she reached the float. She tied her boat and sat on the edge, dangling her feet in the water.

I waved to her and collected the baby from her play pool on the lawn and walked the length of my own dock. The sun was warm. The lake was fairly crowded with the usual preholiday families and sororities. I gave the baby a piece of string to dangle in the water and lay down on my stomach to watch the minnows nibble at the end. The combination of the drowsy hum from the people on the water, the warmth of the sun, and the motion of the minnows was too much for my tired head. I laid it down on my arm and went to sleep.

SEVEN

I was trussed up, hands and feet, to a long, stout pole, and the natives were carrying me through the woods to the sacrificial altar where the High Priest waited with his curved and very dull ceremonial knife. The High Priest was in no hurry; he really enjoyed his work. That rusty blade he waved so energetically was going to take a long time to reach a vital spot.

I was crying sadly, with deep-chested, racking sobs that left my mouth dry, because no one would care too much what became of me. My neck was twisted, my head hanging down. It cut off my breathing.

A voice came to me fuzzily. "Is there anything I can do, Alberta?" I woke sharply, instantly.

The baby was still on her stomach, tempting the minnows with false promises. A hand was patting my shoulder. I recognized Orrin Keller before I turned around.

Rather, I tried to turn. My stiff neck was no dream; both my arms were asleep and were of no use to me as arms. I wet my dry lips and swallowed.

"Don't take it so hard, Alberta. Dear girl." The solicitude in the husky voice could have been spread on a slice of bread.

I rolled over and sat up. Orrin's heavy-jawed, middle-aged face was bent close to mine, his blue eyes concerned, his light and shaggy brows lifted to the limit in his corrugated forehead, pity apparent in every pore. Sitting in the small electric boat brought his face a little above mine. I inched away and hung my feet over the side of the dock.

"I dropped over," he whispered, "as soon as I heard." That was nice, but hardly necessary. I started to say so.

Orrin lifted a smooth, fleshy white hand. "As soon as I heard." He drew a rope through the metal ring on the dock's side and tied the boat fast.

All right, he came over as soon as he heard. That would be the same four-o'clock broadcast Virginia had listened to.

"Is there anything," he went on, "I can do for you and Maggie? In your trouble?"

Our trouble! Wasn't he taking a lot for granted—or—horrible thought—had the radio said anything to implicate Bill? Virginia would have told me.

I tired of looking at Orrin's compassionate and slightly puffy face and turned my attention to his pretty, battery-powered craft. Red leather seats, chromium gadgets galore, varnished wood. Definitely a rich man's toy.

Orrin was obviously waiting for a response. I shook my head.

"Jeannette sends her sincerest sympathy. She'll be over. And she wants you to feel free to call on her—of course she has the house full of out-of-town guests right now—but you feel free. Especially in the next three days."

"Three days!" I said foolishly.

Orrin opened his eyes to their roundest and raised those light eyebrows. "The funeral?"

"Funeral!" I wondered if this was part of my dream. I thought seriously of rolling over on my stomach and trying it all over again. On second thoughts, no; I wouldn't go back to that dream. I shivered, rubbed my arms to smooth out the duck bumps.

Orrin patted my hand paternally. "It's a shame that you and your sister have to go through that again."

Again! I knew people would talk, would remember! I drew my hand away, feeling my face flush.

"Does the boy leave—anything?"

"I don't know," I said. "Police are taking care of all that."

Orrin looked at me steadily, a puzzled frown creeping between the light eyes. "Who does he leave his property——"

This had gone far enough. Orrin Keller was too, too curious. I decided to put a stop to it. I said, "I wouldn't know. I only knew the boy a few days. Not quite a week."

"Not quite a week!" Far from stemming the flow of questions, I had opened the floodgates. "Why, I thought— your nephew—not quite a week!"

I stood my ground, saying nothing, giving him stare for stare. I said firmly, "Bill is my nephew, not Johnny."

"Didn't you tell me——"

I repeated, "Bill is my nephew."

"Well."

"Well what?"

"Tell me—your nephew—Bill——"

"What do you want to know?"

"Why—a——" Orrin made a vague gesture out over the water.

I said, "Bill is all right; Bill is fine."

"Alberta! What are you telling me? The whole lake is buzzing——" He broke off, leaving his mouth open a moment while his facial expression caught up with his thoughts. They made it finally; astonishment making way for commiseration, blue eyes shiny with sympathetic tears.

"My dear girl! You poor child! Am I the one to break—— How can I find——"

I stiffened in spite of myself, heart pounding. "Are you trying to tell me——"

Orrin patted my hand once more, then decided to hold it. "Be brave, Alberta. I'll try——"

I choked. "When?"

"Sometime last night."

"Oh no." I recovered my hand and pushed my hair back off my forehead. Relief kept me tongue-tied. For a few seconds there I'd thought Orrin really had something, something that had possibly happened since the family had left for Old Village.

"He was in the war, wasn't he?" Orrin questioned.

I found my voice. "Orrin," I said, "we're talking about two different boys."

I explained about Bill and his urge to paint. I told him about Johnny, and to make up for the awkwardness Orrin had let himself in for, I went into many details I would otherwise have left out.

Orrin listened breathlessly. He may have liked to dig his own information, but this I was giving him for free he accepted as if it were of his own mining. I described the Blue Place as Max and I had found it. I told him about the progress of the police in the few hours they had been on the case. I even told him about Bill's staying out all night, practically, making a mental note to ask Bill when, exactly, he had gotten in. Must have been very late or very early. Maggie and I seldom sleep through an entry to the house.

Orrin settled back in the red leather seat in the boat and lighted a cigar thoughtfully. He pondered our conversation.

I finally asked him where he ever got the idea——

I had been right. He said, "Radio. Left the city early today on account of the holiday—on the road. Came right over."

I thanked him.

The baby tired of her play and came over and sat in my lap. Orrin gave her an absent-minded smile, leaned forward and pulled a toe. The baby drew her foot away, no answering smile on her face. Orrin asked, "Johnsons'?"

I said, "Yes."

"Cute. Looks like her mother."

I agreed.

After a minute wherein Orrin laid a very businesslike smoke screen with that cigar, he said, "Well, that offer still holds, Alberta. You are likely to be busy in the next few days. Does your nephew's friend leave anything?"

"I haven't inquired," I said.

Orrin reached to the panel before him and turned a key. There was a commotion at the house. Two men came around from the road and made straight for the dock and us. I threw Orrin a pleading look.

"Newspapers," he said. "Want me to do it?" He turned off the motor.

I nodded dumbly. He did it, and efficiently. I thanked him after they went away. He left. I watched him cross the lake; that beautiful boat of his was absolutely the smoothest thing in operation.

Virginia had disappeared completely from the diving float; there was no yellow suit in the crowd splashing and diving around the tower and there was no boat tied to the Lane dock.

The baby and I, hand in hand, moved shoreward; she to her wading pool, I to the glider on the porch. My family came back at the precise moment that Grampie drove in. Mommie collected her daughter and departed kitchenward.

After greeting me, Maggie began battering the pots and pans around in the kitchen. The men stayed out on the lawn and talked awhile. I crossed the porch to the kitchen door and said, "Anything you want me to do, Maggie? How was it?"

"Not bad. Just set the table."

I returned to the glider. The men came up onto the porch; Max to his favorite position, cross-legged on the floor with a beer between his feet. Bill sat in a rocker, one leg hooked over an arm, gesticulating with the hand that held the mate to Max's beer. Grampie sat smoking serenely, a bottle of rye and a shot glass on the railing of the porch at his elbow.

"Well, Bill," I said, "they let you go; I see they didn't try to keep you!"

Max glanced up from under his eyebrows. "By the grace of God and some very fast talking on my part."

"Did I thank you, Johnson?"

"Not properly, but no matter. It was worth it to see you stop sweating. The pool at your feet was threatening a flood. I could feel an undertow."

"Very crumb, that joke. I wasn't nervous!"

"Max!" I scolded. "The boy's been sick."

Maggie came out and spread a cloth on the round table. "Never mind, Bill! Now that Max has taken over, we'll have the—bad man—in no time at all. Behind bars."

Max made a vulgar sound.

I said, "Just how much freedom of movement have you, Max?"

He reached into a small pocket in his trousers and produced a badge. He flashed it so fast that I couldn't read the inscription. It looked official enough. He replaced it with a chortle, and no amount of insistence would bring it out again.

I said, "Well, what does that make you, a chicken inspector?"

"Sticks and stones and all that stuff," Max sneered. "Seriously, I've been sworn in as a deputy, and I am working for and under Troy Ingram. I will not get paid, except in thanks, and I have given my word as a gentleman to take Ingram into my confidence in all important matters."

"I notice," interposed Grampie, "you don't say immediately into your confidence."

Max leered at his father-in-law. "Don't you trust—I've a conscience."

"You wouldn't let it interfere with any private plans you might whip up, would you?"

Max shrugged.

I said, "What are you going to do first?"

"As soon as I finish this"—Max waved his beer bottle— "I'm going out on the lake and think. All by myself."

Maggie spoke from the kitchen. "Not today, you won't. Look at the lake. Tomorrow's a holiday."

We looked at the lake. It was crowded. Small craft. Still no yellow bathing suit on the float. But the skiff was tied to the Lane dock. When had Virginia returned? And why had she avoided us?

I hewed to the line. "What," I asked Max, "are you going to think about?"

"How the heck would I know? I just sit there and turn on the old subconscious."

"Well"—I was persistent—"what do you know? What are you starting with?"

"So you can think about it at the same time?"

I smiled. "We'd never get the same answers."

Max waved both arms. "All right, everyone, what do we know? What have we to start on?" He poured the last of his beer into the glass before him. There was a general, all-inclusive silence. Maggie came to the door and stood there stirring something in a big yellow bowl.

I spoke finally. "Johnny was killed sometime last night by a gun. Before midnight."

"And," added Max, "it must have been someone who hated his guts; pardon my expression, ladies." He broke off to smirk in Maggie's direction, straightened his expression, and continued: "Someone who hated him for his talent, his painting ability."

Maggie said, "That should be easy; just find out who."

Max threw her a look that should have impaled her to the doorframe.

Grampie said, "Did they destroy any——"

"No," Bill said, "because he hadn't unpacked any yet. There was the one he had started——"

"Am I glad I took my things home!" Max hugged a foot. "And you yours."

Bill said, "I won't be needing mine; I'm through. Going to throw them in the lake."

I was tenacious. I said, "Let's get back to Johnny. What do we know about him? I felt a bit on the foolish side this noon—when what's-his-name—— I couldn't tell him anything."

"There's no reason why you should know—should be able to tell them about him." Maggie was out on the porch now. She set the bowl on the table. "Do we have to ask the pedigree of anyone we rent our house to?"

"Certainly not. But the man had a right to expect us to know more than we did. He was a friend of our— of Bill."

Max said, "All right, Bill, tell us what you know."

"I didn't hate him, if that's what you mean," said Bill. "But I'll be honest and say that I was going to move out.

I couldn't have him making——" The young face reddened uncomfortably; he spread his hands, palms outward. "You were all there—I don't have to explain."

The porch was hollow with hush for an uncomfortable few minutes. Finally Bill said, "Say, someone's got to tell her!" He looked from me to Maggie. Maggie shook her head. He was down and off the porch before I could stop him, and he covered the distance across the Johnsons' lawn and to the Lanes' in nothing flat.

I said, "She knows; I told her."

Max said, "These are the possibilities: first, Bill—and he didn't. Second, the blonde, who is probably Johnny's wife if she is driving a Texas car. Third, the usual passer-by. And who ever saw a passer-by in these hills?"

I said, "Have they seen his wife?"

"Nope. No one. Ingram's looking for her. And I'm going to do the same, after I do some thinking and eat some supper."

I said, "There are those trunks to go through at the Blue Place. The police may have run into some enemy."

"Ingram says no. But old Eagle-Eye Johnson will have a go at it tomorrow. Want to help?"

"You know I do!"

Mommie called from her kitchen window, and Max got to his feet reluctantly, because, he said, he thought there was at least one more bottle of beer in the icebox and he hadn't felt that he had his stomach properly lined to take his wife's cooking.

His wife, who is an excellent cook, shouted sweetly, "I heard you, and flattery will get you nowhere. Come home here and dish it out for these kids." Max and Grampie left.

Maggie came to the kitchen door. I set the table finally, and as I was filling the water glasses Bill came up the steps from the direction of the Lanes' looking as if he had been whipped.

Maggie heard him and called from the kitchen, "Go back and get Virginia, Bill. Her mother and father went away this morning, and they never get home from those guild picnics till late."

Bill said, in a voice that left no doubt, "She isn't hungry, and besides, she wouldn't eat at the same table with me."

"What?" said Maggie, showing a surprised face at the door. "Why not?"

"Skip it, Aunt. I was kidding."

Maggie will not be put off when she once gets an idea. "Well, then—go back and ask her."

"No," Bill said rudely. "She really isn't hungry. I asked her." But he lied, and he knew I knew he lied, for he tossed me a pleading look that said, "Don't make me."

Bill, I found out, wasn't hungry either. He might as well not have been at the table. And Maggie had rather outdone herself on this hot, holiday-eve dinner, crisp and crunchy and colorful.

After our coffee and cigarettes Bill excused himself, and I heard the shower running for the second time that day. There was a stirring around sound in his room up over the porch and then quiet.

Maggie and I exchanged a smiling glance as we watched Max, looking neither right nor left, get into the Johnson skiff and, rowing lazily, head toward the middle of the cove.

He had barely cleared the end of the dock when the baby scorched through the screen door, hopscotched down the steps in her own little one-foot-at-a-time bounce that didn't look fast but was, sprinted the length of the dock, and came to an abrupt stop that was a miracle of timing.

She cried out every step of the way, "Daddy, Daddy, Daddy, Daddy."

"Daddy" ignored her, neither decreasing nor increasing his rowing stroke. The eight-year-old followed her down the steps, dignified reproof in her very manner of opening and closing the screen; her usual method being a crash and a bang through and let the slams fall where they may. She proceeded calmly to the end of the dock, and I heard her explaining to the baby in her older-sister-knows-best voice that when Daddy wanted to think he had to go out in the boat to the middle of the lake to find peace and tranquillity. There was too much confusion in the house, and if you went along, why, Daddy couldn't think.

The irresistible impulse of the baby's protests met with the immovable object of the older sister's attitude. Yes, she knew the baby would sit still as a mouse, but no! "Let Daddy think for this one time and then we can confuse him as much as we want in the next few days. He won't be able to say a thing."

The baby, who was merely trying to stall off bedtime, realized that she'd have to work fast if she was to get to stay up a little later. She immediately and good-naturedly abandoned Daddy and looked the field over for other possibilities. She spied Maggie and me at the table on our porch.

Instantly she professed an undying passion for Maggie. She wanted to help Maggie, love, with the dishes. And Maggie, the softie, fell in with her plans to the extent of promising to put her to bed when they were through. She did, too. Both the baby and she enjoyed the routine.

EIGHT

Dusk came. Grampie was established out under the trees on the lawn. Maggie joined him, and they smoked in companionable silence punctuated by mutual congratulations on the fact that they were here, at Ogg Lake, to enjoy the exceptional sunsets, instead of in some horribly foreign place. I was on the verge of asking them what made them think it would be a foreign place if they had been born here? And a sunset is a sunset, isn't it? I bathed and changed my clothes instead and settled myself on the glider once more.

Our cove is a secluded place. The rest of the lake boiled with activity. Across the lake I could see cars coming and going. Speedboats roared senselessly up and down the nine miles that was the length of Ogg. They must moor somewhere. I wondered who would want one, with all its noise. We, in Harris Cove, run to sail and canoe.

Max was anchored out at the edge of where our cove merges into the lake proper, sitting perfectly still, chin in hand, elbow on knee, only changing position to light an occasional cigarette. The speedboats passed and re-passed, leaving violent wakes that tossed the skiff for a few minutes and then diminished, ending in a soft, swishing wave on shore.

The two older Johnson girls came out of the house looking grown up and completely different from the shorts-and-halter-clad youngsters they were in the daytime. In peasant skirts and sheer white blouses, with their hair fluffed about their faces, they looked like the whistle bait they undoubtedly were. They departed for the skating rink at the Point, certain to stop the teen-age show.

Mommie emerged looking not a day older than her daughters, her pretty legs stockingless under her blue sharkskin spectator sports dress. I marveled at her. Four daughters and not a gray hair in that shiny red thatch. I said so from my place on the glider.

"Don't you think it for a minute," she called back. "I'm getting there; found four today. And it isn't from worry or the kids. It's just old Father Time catching up."

She tripped down the steps, letting the screen door slam behind her, and moved across the lawn. "Tell Max," she said, "that I'm going to walk down to the Point with Virginia."

Grampie and Maggie made the proper noises.

"When he's through thinking he might pick me up," she went on. "That is, if he wants a beer. There's none in our icebox, and I think he's cleaned out the Harrises'." She passed behind Grampie's and Maggie's chairs and disappeared into the Lanes' house.

Bill appeared at the living-room door. I said, "You must have fallen asleep."

"Did. The bed looked so darn good after my shower I couldn't resist."

"You look better."

He did, too. Scrubbed and fresh shaven, in slacks and a knit T shirt that showed his good shoulders.

"You look kind of nice yourself." Tribute to my striped chambray; I fancied it took off ten pounds.

"What're you going to do?" I asked.

"Oh, I don't know! Nothing in particular. Thought I'd wait till Johnson gets in and then see what he's planned."

He dropped into a rocker, hooking one leg up over the arm, and kicked the chair into motion. "I should be of some help to him."

We waited for Max.

It was well after nine before he tied the skiff to the dock. He sat and smoked a cigarette with Grampie and Maggie. I joined them and Bill followed me, shrugging into a sports jacket.

"I'm going to get a beer." Max snapped his cigarette out over the lawn.

Maggie laughed. "You'll have to go to the Point for it."

Max twisted in his chair. "You mean some dirty dog——"

Maggie said, "Yes, I mean——"

"Come on," said Bill. "I'm thirsty too."

Max got to his feet. "Anyone else?" He went into his house, appearing immediately bearing a poison-green sports jacket patterned with the loudest plaid I've ever seen.

I got up and followed the two men to the road. We turned toward the Point. As we came abreast of our house I held up my hand; the phone was ringing. I waited an interval for Maggie to answer; she didn't. I said, "Wait."

In Papa's study I took the receiver off the hook and said, "Hello."

Silence. I repeated, "Hello."

"William Hunt?" The voice wasn't right somehow. The speaker was either drunk or wearing a mouthful of hot potato.

I felt a frown between my eyes and I waited, I can't say why, trying to decide whether to hang up or answer.

"I want to speak with William Hunt."

I smoothed out the frown and told myself to stop being silly. I said, "Just a minute." I went to the door to the road and called Bill. He broke off talking with Max. The white blur of his face turned toward me tipped off a warning bell in my subconscious. What had Will said? *He's a sick boy. He's a lot sicker than he realizes. He should be kept quiet; watched fairly close——* The impulse to go back into the study and replace the receiver on its hook was very strong; I hesitated a moment too long. Bill called to me impatiently:

"Who wants me?"

"I don't know," I said. "It's a man, and he's drunker than a lord."

Bill vaulted the hedge and passed me on the steps. I walked around by the gate, and when I reached Max we went on, walking slowly. Bill caught up with us shortly, wearing a thoughtful, puzzled expression.

Max said, "The girl's father? Going to make an honest woman of her?"

Bill shook his head. "Some screwball."

"What did he want?" I asked.

"I don't know."

"Didn't he tell you?"

"He's got me mixed up with someone else."

"Bill," I cried, "you're driving me crazy! What did he say?"

Instantly I was sorry I had asked; I didn't want to know. Our feet slapped against the oiled road, sounding like pistol shots to my suddenly sensate being. There was a silence you could have cut with a knife; a silence that took in just us, had nothing to do with the rest of the world. The cars tore along the main road on our right, the power-boats exploded, put-putting on the lake at our left, the Point ahead of us was a welter of sound; but we three were encased in a capsule of silence.

And without any actual change in the temperature of the air, what had been a soft July breeze became a January chill. The chill crawled in and out, waved up and down like some ectoplasmic monstrosity attaching itself to us as we walked along that familiar, rutty road between Harris Cove and the Point. I felt myself breathing faster.

Bill spoke. " 'Do you want to go the way your friend went last night?' "

Max laughed but he wasn't amused. "What'd you tell him?"

"I didn't get a chance to tell him anything. He didn't want an answer; he was doing all the talking. He said, 'Put that stuff in a paper bag, take it down to the Point, and drop it in the garbage can behind the Penny Arcade. Get that stuff in there tonight, or else.' Then he hung up. That's all."

Max thrust his hands into his pockets and stopped dead still. Bill and I took a couple of tentative steps and then swung around to face Max.

He said, "Hey!"

"Yes?" Bill looked expectantly at Max.

"Let's take that apart before you get any other impressions to——"

Bill nodded agreement.

Max said, "Give it to me all over again."

" 'Do you want to go the way your friend did last night? Put that stuff in a paper bag, take it down to the Point, and drop it in the garbage can behind the Penny Arcade. Get that stuff in tonight, or else.' "

"That's every word he said?"

"Every word."

"Had you ever heard the voice before?"

"Never. Act your age, Johnson. No one knows me—I don't think I've talked over the phone since I've been here, except to Johnny."

"Did he have an accent? Any oddity about his voice?"

"No. But he had his voice muffled somehow."

"You haven't any practical-joking friends?"

"Not here. Home, perhaps. Or college. But that's so long ago—the old gang is scattered—you know."

"It was a local call?" The two men looked in my direction.

I opened my eyes, feeling the look, sensing it; I had had my eyes screwed shut trying to remember, trying to place the one or two words I had heard.

I said hastily, "Of course. A long-distance call has a much longer ring."

"Had you heard the voice before?"

"No. And," I added, "I'm sure he was trying to disguise his voice."

Bill made an impatient gesture. "Why would anyone try to disguise his voice from me? I know no one."

Max thought a minute. "With Abbie, yes. With you, I can't say why."

I shut my eyes again. I had a vision of a nasty, hawk-faced, scrawny old man with a long upper lip distorted over a wad of chewing gum or traditional pebbles. Perhaps he had resorted to a kid trick of a handkerchief over the mouthpiece. I opened my eyes and described him.

Max was sarcastic. "Fine! Now that's settled! We'll look for a man with a long upper lip."

Bill said, "Maybe he merely took out his teeth."

I protested. "I only told you how he sounded to me."

Max and Bill pondered some more, ignoring my latest inanity. Max finally stirred himself and headed toward the Point once more. He spoke to himself. "'Put that stuff in a bag and drop it——'"

Bill and I moved forward with Max. He said, "Well, we'll start at the Arcade. Joe Turner—— Come on!" He quickened his pace, and I found myself running to keep up with them.

The Point at Ogg Lake is the heart and the hub of all lake activity. It is a large tree-shaded area with the hotel on the extreme point, a roller rink on one side, a penny arcade on the other, and a shooting gallery and the usual hot-dog stands scattered about. The hotel boasts a pleasant garden with tables set up on the lawn under the huge cottonwood trees. The dance hall, open on three sides, was near enough so that one could watch the dancers from the tables.

We came abreast of the miniature golf course, gave it not a glance, and turned left to the Penny Arcade. Joe Turner was outside at the popcorn machine. We stopped.

Joe nodded to me and spoke to Max. "Your wife stopped by and got some corn, Johnson. Said you'd pay me. She was with Virginia Lane; they went to the hotel."

Max reached into a pocket and flipped a coin to the man's open palm. "Someday she'll swell up and bust on that stuff you sell. I've told her and told her to keep away!"

"Hey! Have you ever considered doing a murder with your darned old corn? How do we know what you sprinkle on it?"

Joe laughed dutifully. "Let me know and I'll take care of your enemies. You, too, if you have any, Abbie."

I said, "No, thank you, Joe. I haven't any."

"Speaking of murder," Joe said, "did you hear about that lad up in the hills?"

My heart skipped a beat and then raced to pick it up. The thought comforted me that, mercifully, no one connected us with Johnny. He was a stranger. Bless that Troy Ingram! He is a gentleman!

We listened while Joe told the tale, and he was surprisingly accurate. I followed Max's lead and said nothing.

"Been busy tonight?" Max changed the subject.

"Full house; look them over." We looked. The place was full of kids, screaming and milling about among the peep shows, the juke boxes, and the shooting gallery.

"All kids?"

"What grownup in his right mind would go in there? He'd be trampled to death in no time."

It was Max's turn to laugh dutifully. He did. He said, "Who has a phone here at the Point?"

Joe thought a minute. "Up to the hotel. Oh yeah, the roller rink has one to take reservations for big parties."

"Pay station at the hotel?"

"Two, I think. One in the lobby and one in the bar. Why?"

"Got to make a call and don't want to walk back to Abbie's." He might have added that he didn't want eight other parties to listen in.

We left. We walked toward the hotel. Max made a swift detour to the back of the Penny Arcade. When he joined us again he announced, "One garbage can—right."

The bar was crowded. Five deep. We wormed our way to the rail and hooked our arms over the slight ledge. Ed Vincent wiped a space in front of us and said respectfully, "Good evening, Miss Harris."

I had had Ed in eighth grade. I often wondered at the reaction of my former pupils when they see me at a bar. Ed, who wasn't my brightest pupil, looked embarrassed.

Max said, "Hold my beer. I'm going to make a call."

Bill and I held all three. We hadn't long to wait. I said, "I hope Wentis isn't put on this watching detail. He needs his sleep."

Max appeared again. "What are you on, seconds?"

"No," I said. "What'd you do, call Ingram?"

"Right. That garbage can will be watched. Ingram thought it wouldn't hurt. He agrees with me that it was smart to insist on Bill's freedom."

"My freedom is likely to be restricted by a Colt automatic, isn't it?" said Bill. "And if Ingram takes that phone call seriously, perhaps we should."

"I do," said Max. "I take everything seriously at a time like this."

Ed came over. "Hi, Johnson. Heard about the shooting up in the hills?"

"Yep. What do you know about it?" Max had gotten used to the fact that local yokels when they look at him immediately think of crime.

That tendency, I found, isn't confined to the local yokels. I have watched people catch sight of Dr. Custom and immediately talk about operations. And I also. Since seeing Orrin Keller in the afternoon I'd been thinking once more of that watch that needed fixing. But then I, perhaps, came under the heading of a local yokel, having been born there.

Ed was talking. "Just what I hear across the bar. Only been on since eight this evening, so I kind of got caught in the rush. But everybody's talking."

Max drained his glass and pushed it across the mahogany. Ed held it under the spigot and wiped the foam off with his little stick. He gave the glass one more squirt and handed it back to Max.

"Anyone you know? Been in here?" Max asked.

"Naw. Summer customer. But now I think of it, maybe I did take care of him. Stood over there." Ed indicated a point a few feet along the bar.

"We don't get any artists or painters or whatever you call them here at the lake—and when I heard about this artist being shot, right away I thought of this guy last night." Ed broke off to serve two insistent customers on our right.

I wondered what he would call Max. Most likely he hadn't found out Max's new avocation. It certainly had come as a surprise to Maggie and me.

Ed wiped his way back to us. Bill pushed his empty glass toward Ed. He filled it and returned it. "Wouldn't have known he was an artist only he got in an argument with the guy who stood next to him. The other guy got nasty when this artist guy said he was going to leave this section; nothing around here fit to paint."

Max said, "So?"

Ed explained. "So, like I said, the other guy got nasty. 'Best damn scenery in New York State right here, and any damn painter too dumb to see it should get the hell out and go back to the slums where he came from!' Excuse me, Miss Harris."

"What time did this brilliant repartee, this riposte, take place?"

Ed said, "Huh?"

"What time did these—guys—get into the argument?"

"Oh! After I came on. Nine—nine-thirty—around there."

"And . . . ?"

"Nothin'. The painter guy went, but the other guy hung around the rest of the night." Ed moved away.

When he came back to our section Max said, "I hear the police are looking for a blonde from Texas. She staying here at the hotel?"

Ed scratched his head and gave the bar a thoughtful swipe. He covered the lower half of his face with a wet hand and studied the ceiling. "Do Texas chicks talk like Southerners?"

"They are Southerners."

"There are a couple of Southern chickarees staying here. A blonde cha-la and a brunette."

"Are they around where you can point them out?"

Ed grinned. "Pal, if they were around, you could hear them!"

I interposed a question here. I asked, "What time did the shooting story get around here?"

Ed gave it some serious thought before he answered. "I heard it at supper in the kitchen," he said. "But you know how this place is before a holiday. The help is so busy they'd push a dead body under the stove to get it out of the way. It'd lay there, too, till after the rush."

I knew what he meant.

Ed went on, "And the customers! Most of them are feeling no pain now and won't till Monday. God! How I hate holidays."

I touched Bill's arm. "I'm going outside and find Mommie and Virginia. You and Max look us up later?"

"O.K., Aunt." He patted my shoulder and cleared a path for me to the outside of the crowd. I turned at the door to wave, and he was already back at the bar next to Max.

NINE

Outside it seemed comparatively quiet. In reality it wasn't; it was just that there was more space for the noise to scatter. I walked slowly over the grass toward the tables, gulping in the fresh lake smell with deep, right-to-the-bottom breaths.

Mommie and Virginia were seated near the dance hall. I took an empty place, turning in my chair in order to

watch the floor. It wasn't as crowded as it would be later
on. A handful of young couples were making the most of
the space they had, to gyrate in the intricate patterns of
this year's dances. I watched them fascinated, mouth open,
and a little envious. Even though this watching the youngsters dance is a summer-long practice of mine, I never
tire of it. And I never get over being surprised.

"Where's Max?" Mommie said a little impatiently.

"At the bar with Bill." I faced around and put my
elbows on the table.

"Wish he'd get here and pay the bill."

Virginia said, "We're going to look awfully darn silly
sitting here when the sun comes up. And that's what's
going to happen if Max doesn't find us."

"We came off without money," Mommie explained.

"And we didn't want to walk back," said Virginia. "We
were too thirsty."

"He paid for your popcorn," I said.

"Good! He did pick up our trail!"

"He'll be along," I said. We sat in silence and watched
people coming and going for a while. A waiter showed up
and took our order: another beer for Mommie, one for
me, and a coke for Virginia. Mommie asked for a serving of
French fries and I doubled it. When they came they were
nice and hot and salty.

A few people stopped and talked; we greeted others at
a distance, waving. It must have been after ten o'clock by
then; the band had warmed up considerably and the
floor was much more crowded.

At this point I began to feel uncomfortable. I couldn't
explain it to myself. I took my elbows off the table and
studied my companions. Virginia, too, was uncomfortable;
she was positively squirming. Virginia with the flat,

straight shoulders crossed by wide straps of flowered chintz. Virginia, whose slender brown legs under the full skirt were tapping platform-sandaled feet against the table leg. She who had more poise than any dozen girls I know.

Mommie noticed us finally. "What's the matter with you two?"

I said, "I feel as though I'm being stared at."

"Is that what's the matter with me?" said Virginia. "I thought I was making with a nervous breakdown." She laughed with what she fancied was relief.

Mommie smiled. "Don't look now, but you're absolutely right. You are very definitely being stared at, and by none other than Bill's blonde friend. She has her companion with her."

Virginia winced.

We swiveled around, Virginia and I, slowly, deliberately. They were standing in the rear and a little to the right of Virginia, two white-clad women, backs to the dance hall, elbows hooked over the barrier behind them. Very hubba-hubba, and very drunk. They seemed to be scrutinizing Virginia.

That girl spread her hands outward in a gesture of impatience toward Mommie. "Why me? Why not you? They talked to you?"

Mommie grinned and looked exactly like her baby when she has pulled something especially mischievous. "Have you ever seen me with my hair freshly washed and not yet set? They don't recognize me!"

Virginia grinned back, and we swiveled once more to face the two at our backs.

The dark young woman with the alcohol-flushed face spoke in a voice like a poorly adjusted address system, thickly, slurring the words. "Yep, Gladdie! That's Johnny's girl. Think I should push her face in?"

Gladdie, the blonde, but definitely, said, "Naw. Iris, always remember you're a lady."

"And she probably done me a favor."

"Yeah! She done you a favor."

Mommie drew in her breath sharply. I knew she was no longer smiling. I felt her hand on my arm.

Loud-speaker voice repeated, "A great big favor."

Mommie tightened her hold on my arm, and I felt her tense, preparatory to rising.

I took my eyes from our tormenters. The dark one spoke again; the voice was unmistakable. "Should I maybe buy her a drink?"

Virginia showed signs of panic. We—Virginia, Mommie, and I—gazed studiously in the opposite direction.

"Where is that Max?" Mommie cried.

Virginia said, "Couldn't we look for him?"

"And get nabbed for running out on our check?"

"Have you any money?" Virginia said hopefully.

I shook my head. "But I'll sit here till you get back with the men," I offered.

Virginia shot up so quickly she knocked her chair over. She picked it up hastily, hissing across the table, "What'll we do if they follow us?"

Mommie hissed back, "Stop worrying, as long as we get away. We can navigate a lot faster than they; that blonde one is about to fall on her face anyway. Come on!"

I was left alone with three empty bottles, three half-full glasses, and two pairs of eyes boring into my back. I moved around the table to Mommie's place so I could face them. I worried a little about the amount of beer I would have to drink in order to hold the table.

The two women, with drunken fixity, peered after Mommie and Virginia, watching them out of sight. Soberly they transferred their gaze to me. They managed to exchange a look after three or four false tries, seemed to reach an agreement, and with exaggerated dignity wove their way to my table and sat down rather quickly.

"Your daughters?" asked the blonde, showing the whites of her eyes with a toss of her head in the general direction Mommie and Virginia had taken.

Iris tossed her head in an echo and almost threw herself off the chair. She caught the table edge with a clumsy grab at the last possible second. I felt slightly sick.

"Can I help you?" I asked.

Brassy Hair leaned across the table, fingers spread and toeing in, arms akimbo. Her head wagged like a happy, moist-mouthed she-bear. "Lady, we don't need no help."

Red-faced Brunette echoed, serious, bloodshot eyes rubbing against mine like a wet cat, "Never no more."

I wriggled in my chair uncomfortably. She waited for the statement to sink in.

Blonde-girl Gladys took her hands off the table, misjudged the distance, and came within a hairsbreadth of hitting her chin on the edge.

Iris gave her a haughty stare, saying in effect, "Who unlocked the screen and let you in?", swung back, slow-motion, in my direction, and gave me a wise look that explained all. She and I knew how it was! You pick up these friends, but you can't be responsible for what they do in their cups!

I smiled uncomfortably. My face began to hurt a little, keeping the muscles controlled.

"Never no more!" they repeated in chorus, and drifted off on a rosy cloud of speculation.

The band paused; the dancers filed off the floor and immediately on again; the band struck up another number indistinguishable from all the preceding ones.

Gladdie leaned against her companion and whispered. Iris braced herself with her hands, pushed, and managed to get to her feet. She steadied herself against the table, waiting for her companion to find her balance. They launched themselves outward and plowed through the sea of tables like a tugboat towing a tugboat. I watched them go with a distinct feeling of relief. If Max wanted to talk to Johnny's wife, he would have no trouble finding her; he would have trouble getting any sense out of her.

I took a taste of my beer; it was warm. I pushed the glass away and folded my hands on the table. The dance floor was more crowded than ever now. I recognized a lot of people: people who came to the lake every summer; people from Old Village, here for the evening.

There was Frankie Sorbus dancing with a very pretty girl! I waved and he lifted a hand in salute.

Ten minutes later he approached my table, on the oblique as usual, in the manner of a hound dog sniffing a stranger.

I greeted him joyfully. "Hello, Frankie."

"Gol, I'm thirsty! Mind if I sit down?"

"Do," I said. "And I'm not drinking alone, as it may appear. My friends are in the hotel at the moment."

He wrinkled his monkey face in a smile, small blue eyes almost lost in the creases. "I don't like to drink alone either. Have one with me?"

"Thank you," I said, and pushed the platter of potatoes toward him. He took a handful and looked around for a waiter.

Frankie got results. In a very few minutes we had two

fresh bottles and, arms crossed on the table before us, were facing each other chummily.

I began by saying, "Pretty girl you were dancing with, Frankie."

"Sure is!" He poured our beer, downed half of his in one swift swallow, and looked over his shoulder. "Someone else took over for a while, but after this beer I'll have to get back to the party. Sunday-school crowd."

This seemed to require no comment, so I made none.

Frankie lowered his voice to a confidential whisper. "She don't drink."

I looked skeptical. "I didn't know there were any girls left who didn't drink."

"Aw, sure!" Frankie enlightened me, his brows lifting, opening his eyes to their bluest.

"Town girl?"

"You remember her, Miss Harris!" He lowered his brows swiftly. "Connors' girl—Clarabelle Connors."

I remembered her, and sheer astonishment made me impolite. I said, "Of course I remember her! She's a nice girl!" I'm afraid I got the accent on the wrong word.

Frankie didn't seem to mind. He said, "Darn right she's a nice girl! First date I ever had with her was—let's see— at least ten years ago. She was still in high——" Frankie tipped his head on one side and set his glass down. "Nothin' doing then," he whispered huskily, pouring a collar on his beer and tasting it. "Nothing doing ever since!"

We thought it over. Frankie appeared sad but resigned. The statement had seemed fairly final, requiring no comment either. Frankie seemed to be full of statements to-night, like a committee report. And full of confidences.

I said irrelevantly, "How old are you, Frankie? I forget."

"Thirty-six."

"And you never married?"

"Nope!" He creased his face once more in a grin. "Figure it's too late now, Miss Harris."

"Too late!" I exclaimed. "How?"

"Any girl I get now," he breathed huskily, "I'd figure she'd owe me about ten years." His eyebrows shot up and down rapidly, opening and closing his little blue eyes, emphasizing his point. "How are you going to collect ten years of that?"

He had me there. I changed the subject. "Good to see you out of uniform, Frankie. Are you going to stay with Mr. Keller?"

"You bet! Glad to get back, and there's nothing I'd rather do than tinker. And Mr. Keller has plenty of tinkering to be done. The store and his home and the lake place." He drank.

I said, "May I buy you one now?"

"No, thank you, Miss Harris. Gotta get back. Wait'll she smells my breath!"

Frankie Sorbus tipped his bottle into his glass and watched the last fuzzy drops melt into the foam. He turned the bottle upright, lifting his glance to a point above my head, and froze, arm extended. His mouth dropped slightly and the little blue eyes seemed to swell in their sockets, swell and take on the dull fungus growth of fear.

Behind me a voice like hot butterscotch sauce said, smooth and thick, "Sorbus. Frank—Sorbus."

It was a statement, a final statement.

Frankie moved up and out of his chair as a bucket moves from the well when you pull on the rope. He kept the bottle in his right hand.

"Captain—Glenn!" Frankie's whisper had coarsened. Constricted throat muscles had roughened the edges.

"We'll drop the rating, Sorbus." The viscid tones flowed over my head. "You call me Ernie and I'll call you Frank."

My drinking companion and erstwhile confidant swallowed painfully. He made several tries, achieved several failures, and at long last managed a desperate, "Er-Ernie?"

I reached across the table and took the empty beer bottle away from him. I set it down. Then I turned deliberately and examined the man behind me.

I saw a rather fat man, perhaps forty, in a captain's uniform; trim and solid-looking, with a full double chin, a full bold mouth, a pinched, thin nose, full brown eyes under a yet fuller rounded forehead, and thinning, crinkly hair. He held a cap in his hand.

"That's fine—Frank. See you found some civvies. I—haven't taken time. I wanted to see you."

"Me?" Frankie wet his lips.

"You—Frank. As soon as I hit the city this afternoon—I went straight to Keller's Jewelry Store. I talked with Mr. George Keller. I asked for—Edgar Pearson—first, that was. Then—I asked for you. They told me you had just left— to drive Mr. Keller, Mr. Orrin Keller, down to the lake."

"That's right," said Frankie, and managed a ghastly grimace that I suppose he meant for a smile.

"Should we—go somewhere—and have a little talk? Just you and me?"

"Why—yes." Frankie's head jerked to the dance floor, jerked back again as quickly.

"Here with someone?"

"Why—yes. Brought a girl—with a party."

"I can—wait. No hurry for me."

Frankie rubbed the palms of his hands against his trousers. "Wait? . . . Oh! Wait. . . . That's swell—Ernie. You wait."

Ernie cleared his throat, and it was like molasses pouring from a jug—a sort of glug. "Don't mind at all, Frank. Waiting is the best thing I do."

Frankie started to back away, grimacing, bowing, rubbing his hands up and down his thighs.

The thick, ropy voice above me spoke sharply. "Hep!"

Frankie's head snapped up. His mouth opened but he said nothing; he couldn't. He yawped.

"Maybe I could be meeting someone else while I'm here. Maybe I could make some new friend to kill—time."

Frankie's head wobbled up and down as if it were weighted and on a string.

"Want to show me around, Frank, before you join your party? Your girl'll wait, won't she?"

Frankie Sorbus no longer knew I was there. He was strung on a wire, and the fat stranger was jerking the end. He jerked once more, and Frankie stumbled around the table clumsily.

I didn't turn to watch him go. I closed my eyes, putting my hand over them. Nausea that was almost more than I could bear washed over me in wave after wave.

I sat there I don't know how long; it seemed eons. The waves gradually subsided. I began to think about my own immediate circle of friends and wish they would appear. Still I kept my eyes covered. It was restful.

A hand pressed my shoulder, heavily.

I said, "I'll come, Officer." I opened my eyes, expecting Bill or Max. It was Orrin Keller.

"What are you—— Abbie!" He looked embarrassed and sat down quickly. "Wish—I could help you." His face was puckered with concern, and I began to feel sorry for him. Then it struck me funny and I laughed.

"Drowning my sorrows in drink? Is that what you

think I'm doing?" Laughter was a release; I guffawed. There were perfectly normal people in this world after all! Orrin—stuffy, dull, commonplace Orrin Keller—looked so good to me I could have wept. I laughed again and long and patted his hand.

He laughed back at me, with me, dutifully. "Well—er —no."

"Don't try to get out of it, Orrin. That's exactly what you meant. What would you like me to do?"

"Now, now, Abbie! You've got me all wrong. I realize now the boy was nothing to you. He wasn't, was he?"

Wonderful, irritating, heavy-thinking Orrin! Leave it to him to twist any conversation around to a series of questions by Orrin and answers by someone else! I didn't care. Just ask, Orrin! I'd be glad to answer.

I said, "No, he wasn't. You do mean Johnny Rutland? Do I sound heartless? I suppose I should—— Well—after all, he was alive and now he's dead!"

"Painter fellow, wasn't he?"

"Yes."

"Eccentric class."

I didn't know; I hadn't had any experience with artists.

"Any good?" Orrin asked.

"Good enough to have some stuff hung," I explained. "In Washington."

"Well, what do you know." Orrin thought that over.

We were silent for a while. It was a pleasant, companionable silence. The waiter appeared, and Orrin ordered a scotch. I refused another beer. I began to dread getting to my feet; I'd have to be launched shortly myself.

Orrin leaned across the table. "So he was a friend of your nephew's?"

I brought myself back from an imaginary swim in a

lake of beer; I was in no condition to hold my own against Orrin and his curiosity. I resigned myself to answering meekly. But, I promised myself, I didn't have to be truthful. The too-curious deserve deception.

"So he was a friend of your nephew's," Orrin repeated. "What theater did your nephew——"

"Pacific," I anticipated him.

"Pacific, eh? Did this painter fellow—was he——"

"Yes."

"Didn't he get to the European——"

"Bill?"

"Is that his name?"

"My nephew?"

Orrin produced a handkerchief and wiped his forehead. His heavy face wrinkled in that let's-begin-again expression.

"Your nephew's name is Bill?"

I smiled sweetly and nodded. He seemed to be satisfied for the moment. Shortly his face clouded as another problem presented itself.

"I thought you said your nephew painted?"

"He did," I said. "For one day."

Orrin frowned, concentrating. "Wasn't he with that unfortunate fellow? The other night?"

"Thank goodness, no," I answered.

Orrin tasted his drink, barely wetting his lips. "Heard it was quite a mess."

My stomach tipped at the remembrance. Once more I said nothing, nodding my head and casting my glance right and left, hoping I'd catch sight of my neighbors. Hadn't I gone into all this this afternoon? Orrin wasn't only a stupid bore, he was a ghoul. Where were Mommie and Virginia, Max and Bill?

Orrin said, "Lots of property destroyed?"

I said, "Bill was lucky, and so was one of our neighbors, Max Johnson." I added to myself that their luck was rapidly running out. If they didn't show up soon, I'd show them what property destruction was—a mere nothing to what would happen to them.

"Lucky?" Orrin appeared interested. "Why?"

"Because Bill saved his nice new paint set by putting it into the trunk of his car instead of leaving it in the house. And so did Max."

"The trunk of——"

"His car," I finished for him.

"I don't see how——"

I began again. "Bill, my nephew, instead of putting his paints into the house at the end of the day—they were working in the old orchard that day—put them into his car and drove off. They're still there, for all I know. Whoever killed Johnny didn't leave a whole tube of paint."

"So I heard," said Orrin. "Must have been crazy."

"That's what the paper said: 'The work of a maniac.' "

Orrin got to his feet quickly, saying, "Good evening."

Mommie dropped into the chair opposite me. I rolled my eyes heavenward. She kicked me under the table.

"Hello, Mr. Keller. Abbie, I found him. But I had trouble getting him away from the bar." She twinkled up at Orrin. "That husband of mine sticks to mahogany, somehow."

"Only if it's elbow high and horizontal," explained Max. "Hello, Keller." They shook hands.

Orrin reached for his drink and tossed it off. "Have you seen Jeannette about?" he said. "She'll be looking for me."

"She's right over there." Mommie indicated a large party at a long table near the water. How long had they been there? And what did they think of their host spending the time he did at my table?

Orrin sat down again. "I guess she's in good company. All our own week-end guests."

"Where are Bill and Virginia?" I asked.

"Dancing." Max reached over the table and picked up my beer. "Guy don't know when he's well off."

I exclaimed, "What!"

Mommie nodded confirmation. "Aren't they funny?"

"Why—why, she wasn't speaking to him at dinnertime!"

"Remind me to tell you all about it, Abbie. Ginnie has the——"

"Poor fish," Max interjected.

Mommie made a mouth at her husband. "Shut up." She leaned toward me. Max stood there and poured a carefully measured drop of beer on her head. "They said to go on home without them. They're going to dance a few and then walk back to the cottage and go for a ride in Bill's car."

"With the top down," augmented Max. "Virginia has decided that the moon is right for the top down."

Mommie brushed the beer off her head. "And Virginia was all for seeing the place where Bill ran out of gas last night."

"Silly excuse to get the guy to herself for the express purpose of befuddling him."

"She's got something there," said Orrin, rising. "A night like tonight?" He looked up at the star-sprinkled sky. "She shouldn't need an excuse."

"Just a befuddler," stated Max.

Orrin bowed. "Well, good evening, all. It was nice having a talk with you, Alberta. We must see more of each other this summer. Jeannette said so the other day." He left.

"I'll bet!" said Mommie, with Orrin passing rapidly out of earshot.

"Those who aren't befuddlers are cats," Max announced to the world around him, not looking at either of us. He signaled to the waiter.

The bill brought a groan, from the very depths. He paid it and we walked home, stopping long enough behind the Penny Arcade to greet the officer who was on the job there. It wasn't Wentis.

TEN

I've read how life began on this planet, and I don't have to wonder how it feels to struggle up out of the quagmire fighting for the chance to evolve and live. I must undergo an atavistic change when I sleep, for being wakened from that first deep sleep is a ghastly experience: I go through all the changes from slug to reptile to mammal, and it isn't easy.

Maggie and I fell exhausted into our respective beds; it had been one long day, tiresome and enervating. And sleep hit me like a house falling onto my head. I went out like a bonfire in a cloudburst, barely conscious of Bill and Virginia talking under my window, getting into Bill's car and driving off.

It was perhaps a million years later that I went through the painful process of waking. The phone was ringing. It was dark or I was blind, and I found myself halfway downstairs clutching a light robe over my head, as if I were going out into a snowstorm, before I realized it was the phone. I had been under the impression that the house was on fire.

I let go of the robe and lifted the receiver to my ear.

"Abbie?"

"Yes."

"Bill!"

"Yes," I said a little crossly. It wasn't Bill's voice but Virginia's, I thought. And while I, too, liked Bill and was glad she did, I certainly wouldn't have called her up to tell her so. I repeated, "Yes?"

Nothing; the wire went dead. And had I really heard a short exhalation, as if the speaker had put her mouth against the phone? And had there been a dragging sound?

The robe slipped off my head and slithered to the floor, making a small puff of wind that chilled. I was awake—horribly, fearfully awake. I clawed the wall phone before me, trying to shake some life into it.

"Virginia! Virginia! Where are you?"

A slight scratching sound was all the answer I got.

"Virginia!" I jiggled the hook desperately.

Jake Meyers, the night operator, answered me in a sleepy voice. "Your party hasn't hung up, Miss Harris. I'll keep your lines open. Maybe she'll come back."

"Where's she calling from?" I shouted.

"Hill's garage, I think. That line, anyway."

"Jake," I cried, "can't you make some noise there?"

"Not unless they hang up."

We both listened; I could feel Jake listening; I could almost hear him put on the headphones. Out in the country as he is, he doesn't wear them in the night; calls are few and far between.

There was a distant scrabbling sound. I hung on, staring at the black mouthpiece, hugging it with my hand, as if using my sense of feeling and sight would augment hearing.

Maggie appeared at my side and mercifully kept silent.

There were more noises, a voice. Finally a weak "Hello."

I almost sank to the floor with relief.

"Virginia?"

"I'm sorry—Abbie. I seemed to have fainted. The man—kind enough to help me."

Maggie breathed down my neck gustily. I gestured and she moved away.

"Virginia! Tell me! What about Bill?"

"He's—hurt. Oh, Abbie, I was all right—till I heard your voice——"

"Go on."

"He's hurt—bad."

"Where are you?" I demanded. "At the hospital?"

"Oh no! I'm at a gas station. Bill's lying—— Oh, Abbie!"

"Virginia! Now stop it! Tell me—tell me all I should know!"

There was a choking sound. "He's down the road, and I walked—ran—here—the first place I saw, and I made him wake up—— Oh, Abbie, I thought I'd never make him hear me!"

"Go on."

"So he showed me the phone and I got you. I don't know how badly—but you—I knew you'd take care——" Virginia's voice was high and hysterical.

Once more I said sternly, "Stop it! Now tell me where you are exactly, and I'll take over."

There was a shuddering sigh and a slight pause while the girl organized her thoughts. She said finally, "Go up the lake road to the head of the lake."

"Yes."

"Turn right and drive across the head of the lake till you hit the other lake road. Know where I mean?"

"Yes."

"Turn left—you know how that road climbs the hills?"

"Yes."

"I don't know how far away I am—Bill and I weren't watching the road. I think we went over two hills."

"Go on."

"The man here will keep his light on—he'll tell you how to find us. Hurry, won't you, Abbie?"

"Of course, darling."

"I've got to get back to——" Her voice rose once more.

I said, "Get back, Virginia, and I'll take care of everything." But I spoke into a dead phone. Virginia had hung up and left.

I put the receiver back on the hook and looked at my sister. Blue eyes wide open and white head tousled, she stared back at me, waiting. I said, "Bill's been hurt."

She bobbed her head up and down, still not speaking.

I said, "I'll wake Max and we'll get out there. You call Dr. Custom and tell him this: go out the lake road to the head, cross the head of the lake to the other lake road, and turn left. Follow that road till he sees a gas station open, and the man there will direct him. It's near, according to Virginia."

Maggie, the efficient, repeated my directions.

"Better call Ingram," I added. I picked up my robe and slipped my arms into the sleeves. I tore out of the study door and across the lawn to the Johnsons'.

The screen door was locked, which surprised me. I had no idea that any of the lake people locked their doors. I picked up a handful of pebbles and ran back to do the traditional against the bedroom window. It took three tosses.

Max stumbled out onto the upper porch wearing a pair of pajama pants. He growled. I told him about the call, briefly, and raced back to my own house without waiting. I knew he'd take over without my asking, and time was of the essence.

By the time I had thrown on a dress and scrambled down the stairs again, Maggie was through explaining to Dr. Custom and had started on Ingram. She was shivering visibly, and I put an afghan over her shoulders.

Max was already out on the porch and headed in the right direction, engine running. I fell into the seat beside him. We said very little on the lake road. Making those intricate curves with his foot pressed to the floor boards kept Max fully occupied. The holiday visitors who had had to leave their cars parked at the side of the road created an additional hazard that, had my hair not been gray, must have made it so.

We turned right at the head of the lake. Max asked me to repeat the story. I did.

We arrived in nothing flat, I'm sure, at the other lake road. Max, turning left, settled back a bit for the home stretch. And there was the lighted garage.

A bald-headed man in a greasy pair of dungarees shot out of the door when the brakes squealed, leaned into the window, and started shouting directions. He looked as if he had gone to bed without washing.

"Down the road to the first crossroads. Right there you'll find her. I didn't want to let her go back alone, but she insisted. No one here to show——"

Max pulled away, snatching the door handle out of his grimy, broken-nailed hand. He went up, not down, the road, climbing another hill and going a little slower so as not to pass the crossroads. I recognized this stretch of road as a very beautiful part of our hill country in the daylight. At night it proved to be a little sinister, a little terrifying, dangerous. We came to the crossroads and Max applied the brakes.

Virginia called us from the ditch.

Actually it wasn't a crossroads; the side road didn't cross. It led off to the right, downhill, steeply. And Bill's car lay on its side in the ditch. Max and I jumped out and ran.

The car lay, nose down, on its right side. Bill had evidently been thrown over the windshield; he lay on his back, his head pillowed on Virginia's lap, breathing stertorously. She stared up at us, white-faced and frightened.

"I thought you'd never come."

"Got here as soon as we could." I knelt beside my nephew and touched his face. Max dropped to the ground on the other side.

Virginia said, "His eyes are open, but he doesn't know a thing."

His eyes were open, horribly, and his mouth hung slack and bubbled with his hoarse breathing.

Max rose, went over to the car, and played the beam of his flash over it.

"Here's where he hit him." With tender fingers Virginia touched a spot behind Bill's left ear.

Max whirled on us. "He hit him? I thought——" Virginia looked up into the beam of the flash, eyes enormous in a white face. She nodded.

A siren sounded in the distance, and Max raced to the main road, waving the flash.

I said, "Who?" I picked up one of Bill's limp hands and held it.

Dr. Custom leaped out of the car that swung, with

screaming brakes, off the main road and came to a nerve-shattering stop next to Max's. "Leaped" isn't quite the word for Dr. Custom; his legs aren't long enough. He bounced. He arrived quickly with his little black satchel and his understanding hands and his handsome face like a thunder-cloud.

Ingram followed, said hello to us, and went directly to Bill's car. Dr. Custom was shouting:

"What in hell's going on here? What'd you move him for?"

He grunted as he lowered his weight to his knees, opened his satchel at his side, and pulled out his stetho-scope, hooking it around his short neck. He picked up a limp wrist and looked at his watch.

"I didn't move him!" Virginia's dirt-streaked face flew up and glared at the little man fiercely. "I held his head. To see if he was breathing." She slid out from under the head in question and lowered it gently to the ground and stood up. She started to take a step, stumbled, and would have fallen if Max hadn't caught her.

"Are you hurt, Virginia?" Max asked.

"I—don't think so." She clung to him. "I walked—I even ran—I couldn't run—could I?"

Virginia seemed to be talking, just talking; neither caring nor aware of what she was saying. She was watch-ing, with terror-widened eyes, the little doctor who was going over the big young man carefully, inch by inch, limb by limb, not missing a muscle, a joint; probing in the soft parts of his body, ending the search at his head again. He shouted at Max for more light. Max turned the beam of his flashlight on Bill's face. Dr. Custom peered into the wide-open eyes.

He stood up, complaining loudly at the effort. He gave us his verdict. "Not a bone broken, not a muscle swollen, no bleeding. Just that blow behind the ear. Who did it?"

"A man." Virginia had the undivided attention of us all. Ingram walked over, abandoning his inspection of the over-turned car and the ground surrounding it.

I said, "Never mind who did it! What are we going to do for him?"

"We get him home," said Dr. Custom. "He'll come to any minute now. An hour, usually, for concussion." He swung on Virginia. "How long ago did this happen?"

"I—forget, Doctor. The man drove away after—after he went through Bill's car. Then—I crawled over to Bill. Then—I went up the road till I found the gas station——" Tears started, making the brown eyes shiny. She tried to smile. "I had such a time getting him to waken—then I called Abbie." The tears overflowed the eyes, making tracks on the dirty cheeks.

The doctor was down on his knees again. I faced him across the limp body. "Don't you worry, Abbie, we'll take care of him. He's young and healthy."

I swallowed twice before I found my voice. "That's just the trouble. Is he?" I groaned. "I don't know how I'll tell his father."

Ingram had gone to the main road and backed his car down to us. He opened the back door. "Think we can get him in on the seat?"

"Right." Max approached the unconscious Bill, followed by Ingram. Max took him carefully under the shoulders and lifted. His head lolled heartsickeningly. Ingram seized him by the knees and they bent to the task of moving him.

There was a convulsive jerking in the supine Bill, and quicker than it takes to tell it, Ingram was sprawled on his face on the ground and Max was defending himself from a maniac bent on complete annihilation. The boy had come to life and he had come up slugging.

Ingram jumped to his feet and Max's aid. They had all they could do, the two of them, to pin the boy down on the ground again. I screamed and covered my eyes. It was over in a minute.

Virginia was at his head again instantly. "Bill! Bill! Are you all right? Bill, say something."

Bill still thrashed spasmodically, but his heart wasn't in it. Max was talking to him in that low, deep, resonant voice of his, steadily, monotonously. Made you feel that everything was going to be all right.

Dr. Custom dropped, complaining, to his knees once more. "Thought for a minute we'd have to slug you on the other ear," he said. "Going to behave, or must I give you the old shot in the arm?"

Bill seemed not to be able to talk. He made a few guttural noises. His eyes were closed now and he was moaning a little. Virginia was still as close as she could get, still saying his name in tones that, had he been in a state to understand them, would have been gratifying. He opened his eyes.

Dr. Custom said, "Now, don't talk unless you feel you have to, lad."

"I—can't—see."

"That's all right."

"No—it—no!"

"What I mean, boy—you've had a nasty blow. But when the effects wear off, you'll be able to see." The little man groaned dolefully but managed to get to his feet. "Now, young fellow," he said, "we'll get you home and into bed, and I don't want you to do any talking. Unless it's to

Ingram. You've just so much strength, and I want you to save it for the Law."

Bill turned his face toward the booming voice above him, started to shake his head and thought better of it. Max and Ingram helped him upright and to the car. Virginia climbed in first and quite normally indicated her lap as the proper place for his head. He let her guide him.

I sat in the front seat. Max got behind the wheel. Ingram came up to the window. Max said, "You want me to call Wentis and have him come down here and relieve you?"

"Right. I'll get the photographers here in the morning. No use getting them out of bed. It's not going to rain or anything." He moved to Virginia's window. Max turned the key and touched the starter. Ingram said to Virginia, "Don't go to bed, young lady. As soon as Wentis gets here I'll be around to take your statement. And Hunt's too, if the doctor'll let me." We drove off.

ELEVEN

Bill was in bed and glad to be there. Dr. Custom had given him the promised sedative, and Max and Ingram were working against the time when it would take effect. Virginia sat on the bed, leaning against the foot; she had refused to go home when Maggie had insisted.

"Mr. Ingram wants to ask me questions, and besides, I'm not going to wake Mother and face a lot of questions from her. I want to get it all over with at once and then go home and sleep for a week. By the way"—she turned to the little doctor in the doorway—"don't I get anything to quiet my nerves?"

Dr. Custom said, "Hold out your hand. No, the other side up. Now, straight out."

Virginia held her right hand out at arm's length, and it was as steady as if it were carved of stone. There was a chorus of laughter.

Dr. Custom went downstairs, demanding coffee of Maggie. He got it. And a piece of strawberry shortcake. Don't ask me how Maggie does it!

Ingram said, "Now! You do the talking, Virginia, and you interrupt, Hunt, if she gets anything wrong."

Virginia put a hand to her forehead, shut her eyes. After a moment she opened them and used both hands to smooth out her chintz skirt. "We left the Point about eleven and walked to the house. We got into Bill's car."

Ingram interrupted. "Was anyone following you?"

Virginia consulted Bill with her eyes. He shook his head, but carefully. She said, "No. We didn't notice."

Ingram nodded.

"Well," she went on, "we got into the car, Bill had the top down, and we drove off. That's all." She spread her hands in a palm-up motion and smiled at the assembly.

Ingram said, "Still no one following you?"

Again Virginia looked at Bill. A frown appeared between her straight brows. "That's hard to say. The crowd breaks up at the Point, you know, about that time. Cars were leaving. Some in front of us, some behind."

"Yes?" Max said.

"We drove slowly up the east side of the lake. There was quite a bit of traffic—you know how the lake is before a holiday. People going back and forth to each other's cottages."

"Was there any car that stuck close to you?" Max asked.

Virginia frowned again. "I don't think so—we didn't watch. We turned off at the head of the lake—I told you——"

"I know," said Ingram, "but I want to hear it again."

Max said, "Where did the car come from?"

Virginia consulted Bill once more. Bill made a few tentative noises and then spoke.

"Honest to John, I don't know where it came from! There we were, doodling along fairly slowly. It's hilly, and we just got over the rise in the road when it happened! From nowhere! First—there is just a little hill on my left" —he gestured—"and a downslope on my right." His hand indicated the floor on his right. "The road rolling before me, all clear, and I suppose all clear behind me. I don't remember headlights in the rearview mirror.

"Next thing I know, this bird swoops over the hill from behind and squeezes me. No lights.

"I step it up a little; I realize now I should have slowed —I see this side road leading down, so I swing that way and still he squeezes.

"I knew we would turn over in that second before it happened—but what could I do then?"

Virginia took up the tale, eyes bright in her still-dirty face. "It sounds like slow motion, but believe me, it happened fast! One minute we're rolling along the road, and the next I have my mouth full of ditch weeds. I don't move, 'cause I can't, but I open one eye and what do I see?

"There is a man leaning over Bill and does he help him up? No! He hits him on the head with—well, with something!"

Max said, "And you didn't yell?"

Virginia shook her head vigorously. "For the first split second I was too astonished and after that too scared. I just lay there and peeked out of one eye. I shut that when I thought—he—was looking at me."

I said, "I wonder why he didn't hit you?"

Bill winced.

Virginia said, "He didn't. He came over and looked at me a couple of times. I was on my face and too covered with dirt——" She held out her once-pretty chintz skirt. It looked as if she had been dragged by a rope from the back of a car along a dirt road. "You see," she went on, "I kind of slid out of the car when it tipped. Like I used to on the baseball team when I made third base."

"Did he touch you?" asked Ingram.

"Oh yes. My shoulder. He gave it a little shake."

"Go on."

"He went right back to Bill and went through his pockets."

Max said, "Did he take anything?"

"I don't think so."

Bill nudged Virginia with a foot. "You didn't play it right, sister. Why didn't you fire from your hip?"

"Listen, goon, I was too scared! Anyway, I told you I was lying on my stomach."

Ingram asked, "Tell us what he looked like, and what did he hit Bill with?"

"He was big."

"How big?" asked Ingram.

"I don't know—just big."

"Didn't you see his face?"

"I couldn't. He carried a flashlight. Kept it in front of him. He had gloves on—white canvas gloves. That I remember because he kept taking them off for some things, like going through Bill's pockets, and putting them on for others, like when he went through the car."

Max said, "Probably conked Bill with the flashlight. Makes a beautiful concussion!"

Ingram nodded. "Gloves take care of fingerprints. How was he dressed, Virginia?"

"I think a long raincoat—or a reversible. Something light-colored. I told you," she complained, "I told you I was on my stomach. What can you see from your stomach?"

"Tell us exactly what you could see of him."

"Pants, raincoat, brown shoes."

Max said, "And you couldn't see his face?"

"Goodness no. I had only one eye out, and as I told you, he kept the flashlight in front of him."

"No car lights?"

Virginia shook her head. "The lights on our car must have gone out, and he didn't have any."

Ingram said, "What made you decide to play possum—not defend Bill—call for help?"

"I can't say, really. Instinct, I guess. When the man hit Bill I realized he had run us off the road and wasn't just a crazy drunken driver. I thought I'd wait and see. And I had the feeling the man wasn't alone."

"What!" exclaimed Ingram.

"I thought," said Virginia, "I thought once of crawling along on my stomach in the ditch and getting away that way—but—I realized I wouldn't get far—he kept coming back and looking at me."

Max sat up straight. He had been hunched over his legs crossed on the floor. He blanked his cigarette in the tray between his knees and said softly, "Who?"

Bill looked surprised in a sleepy, can't-keep-my-eyes-open way. "How do you know?"

Ingram stopped and leaned against the headboard, facing Virginia. "Say that again! Did you see the others, and how many? One—two—three? A gang?"

Virginia's pretty face puckered up with the effort. "I

can't think! I think I heard other footsteps, but they didn't talk. The man who hit Bill kept looking up as if he were consulting someone as to what he should do next."

Ingram expelled his breath and dropped his hand from the headboard. "So—you can't say how many? You didn't see anyone? But you're sure there was at least one more person with the man?"

Virginia nodded. "I could feel them walking—the ground shivered—you know what I mean."

Max lighted another cigarette and slumped down again. "Go on, Virginia. What'd he do next?"

"I think he went through the car. Or someone else was going through the car—yes—I'm sure now—while the one man was going through Bill's pockets, someone was going through the car. There were a lot of tinny sounds."

Bill opened heavy-lidded eyes, "I beg your pardon."

Virginia gave him a dirty smile that showed her even white teeth. She patted his feet and he closed his eyes again.

She said, "He went back to Bill and then he went away. Hey—I'm surer and surer there were other people around. I heard more than one door close before they went away."

Ingram pressed a hand to his eyes. "How long'd you wait?"

"Till I heard the car turn onto the main road."

Max said, "See anything?"

"I raised up to my knees. I was afraid to jump right up—I saw a big dark car driving off toward the lake."

"License?" Ingram took his hand down from his face.

"No. No lights; I told you that. Bright moonlight—a big dark car—coupé, I'd guess."

Max moaned, "If only you'd gotten the license!"

"But Bill!" Virginia wailed. "I was thinking about him! He might have been dead! I got over to Bill and—he was breathing. You know the rest."

Max looked up at Ingram, still at the head of the bed. He transferred his gaze to Bill. "Anything to add to that, Hunt?"

He had to call him again. "Bill."

Bill opened his eyes sleepily. "Huh?"

"Anything to add to what Virginia has told us?"

Bill wrinkled his forehead in the effort to think. "No—nothing—except that I could hear a lot of what was going on around me before I could do anything about it. But that was after—about when you arrived. And I was darned scared when I couldn't see!"

Max and Ingram smiled at each other. "We know," said Max.

Dr. Custom yelled from up the stairs, "When are you going to get out and let that lad rest? He's going to feel some shock tomorrow as it is, and I'm going to call for him about ten o'clock. Got a nice date with a nice little X-ray machine in the hospital. Now git!" He slammed the door and departed.

TWELVE

I was up at seven and by seven-thirty had eaten and was on the lookout for Max. I wanted to go along when he went to look at the car in daylight. And I felt sure he was going to do something about the Blue Place. He was.

"Where are you going first?" I asked, seating myself in the front beside him.

He looked sidewise at me, as though I were in the last stages of leprosy, and gripped the wheel, making no move to start the car.

"Yes," I said, "I'm going. So get used to the idea. Where to, first?"

"Why?" He groaned. But he pressed the starter.

"Never mind why. Just say I'm interested."

"There is another and less lovely word for it," he said through grated teeth. He gunned the car out onto the road as if he were going to take off and fly. We started up the lake road. We drove the whole way in silence. I regretted not having asked Max to share my breakfast. Hunger makes any male cross, I realized.

In silence we climbed out of our separate sides when we reached the overturned car. Ingram was there before us, Ingram and three others.

"What have you found, Ingram?" asked Max. He didn't explain my presence, and Ingram didn't seem curious.

"Not a thing. Some blue paint on the fender, that's all. Dark blue paint. No tracks to speak of. The skid marks are Bill's. Look at this road," he said disgustedly. "Boulders."

It was cold up here in the hills. I climbed back into the car and put up the window on the driver's side. I hugged myself to keep warm.

The view was superb. The road before me dipped steadily south for miles and miles, then swung a little east and climbed another series of wooded hills. Over to my right, in a fold of three hills, I could see the roof tops and inevitable church steeple of a village glinting in the eight o'clock sun.

In the foreground were scattered innumerable farms, white houses, red barns, and silos turned silver. Squared-off fields held grazing cattle. Men were moving in other fields, men riding high-seated tractors, men atop loaded hay wagons. Holiday came second to farm work, especially in haying season.

Max and Ingram came back from a minute inspection of the road behind me. Max climbed in behind the wheel

and ran the window down. Ingram hooked his arms companionably over the edge.

Max said, "I'm going up to the Blue Place and look
around. Who's there?"

"Disbrow. Let me know if you get anything."

"Right," said Max, and we drove away.

We retraced the way to the lake in absolute silence once
more. "What do you think?" I asked brightly as we swung
off the lake road and started to climb again.

"I don't think. It's much too early. I never think while
I'm driving a car, and I especially don't think when I don't
have all the facts."

I said, "That's ridiculous. You can't get all the facts
unless you do some thinking."

"All right, then, what do you think?"

He had me there. What did I think? There was little to
go on that made sense. First Johnny and then Bill. I
summed it up. "This is all I know, and I'll keep to facts.
Johnny was shot and the house torn up as though someone
had had a temper tantrum. Like a woman who was good
and mad."

Max said, "And Bill?"

I rubbed my eyes; they prickled with lack of sleep. "I
can't see why—— Bill! Bill! That awful blonde!"

Max nodded and swerved sharply to avoid a small brown
bunny. I went back to women. "Remember that woman in
last week's paper who wished she had hit her husband with
a frying pan instead of a coffeepot?"

Max nodded again. "So you think it was his wife?"

"Yes," I said. "She is obviously one of those egocentric
drunks—capable of all kinds of violence."

"Where'd she get the gun?"

"Why—right there in the trunk! It was in the top drawer

of that wardrobe trunk that stands between those windows."

"Did you see this gun?"

"You don't think I'm making this up?"

"No. But I've encountered your imagination before."

"I saw it—the gun, I mean."

"What did she do with it?"

"You and Ingram will have to find out. Don't tell me Ingram hasn't done anything about her——"

Max took a hand off the wheel, reached into a pocket of his jacket, and selected a cigarette. He shot me a withering blighting glance from his hooded brown eyes that were a little pink where they should be white. He lighted his cigarette. After the first puff he spoke.

"That dame got herself up to the office—Ingram's—as soon as she heard the broadcast. She's after the insurance and whatever else he owned, and she'll take care of the body when Ingram releases it. That is, if she sobers up sufficiently."

"She has an airtight alibi—she and her blonde friend. They covered the bars around the lake on the night in question—very conspicuous, the two of them. They picked up and got rid of no less than three men apiece."

Max chuckled to himself. "Ingram's men have tracked them down and brought them in for questioning, all six of them, and at no little embarrassment to all six." Max laughed aloud.

I said, "Has he looked for a gun on her?"

Max shook the ash from his cigarette out of the open window. "But natch! And her room at the hotel—though that last you'll keep to yourself."

I hated to give that hussy up as my choice for the murderer. Max read my mind.

"Now, Abbie! You're going to have trouble making her into Virginia's big bad man in the raincoat."

"I don't know!" I was stubborn. "She could have had an accomplice. Her blonde friend?"

Max said, "This is more than just a jealous killing. Use your head, Abbie! I know Ingram said that nine out of ten murders have sex at the bottom of them—but this may be the tenth. Must be. Obviously someone is looking for something."

I said, "Oh!"

We climbed Marrowback Hill, Max's car protesting a little. Max said, "I'm going to look over the house once more, then I'm going to go home and snatch some sleep, and when I wake up I'm going to find myself a nice quiet place and do some real thinking."

He tossed his cigarette out on the macadam of the main road before he turned the car into the side road where the sign said "Dead End." A young man got up from the bank on the side of the road and held up a hand. Max stopped. He said, "Johnson."

The young man smiled. "Heard you lost some sleep last night."

"Right. Many people get through?" Max indicated the shady road ahead.

"No one gets through. But lots of folks try. Along about noon they start coming, and they don't give up till after dark."

We drove on and pulled up in front of the house and directly behind a police car that evidently had the two-way radio working: I could hear squawkings and squealings. Disbrow got up from the steps where he had been sitting, dropped his cigarette and stepped on it. He greeted Max and gave me a sidelong look. I said hello to him and he answered, but reluctantly. I began to feel like excess baggage, but I tagged along just the same. We went into the house.

Someone had cleaned up. At least had straightened. The paint still streaked the windows, but it had been wiped up from the table and floor. All the messy stuff had been gathered and placed in cardboard cartons under the window. Max went directly to these and dropped to his heels. He handled the drying, mutilated tubes, shaking his head a little mournfully. "Why," he asked himself, "would anyone want to destroy these?"

Of Bill's clothes there was very little. He hadn't moved any of his dressier things from his room in our house. A pair of pajamas, a few pairs of slacks, T shirts, clean socks and underwear. A razor and toothbrush, a camera. Nothing too personal.

Wentis lost interest in a job that had doubtless been done again and again by the police. He returned to his place on the porch steps.

Max went to the wardrobe trunk between the north windows. Johnny's possessions shrieked money and revealed a fastidious nature that I found hard to tie up with his choice of the woman who claimed to be his wife. Toilet articles the like of which I hadn't seen outside the pages of *Esquire*. Fine, soft underwear, twenty-dollar woolen shirts, hand-knit socks and ties that took my breath away. He must have been out of his mind and his class when he had bound himself to that red-faced creature who would collect his insurance. I said so to Max.

Max nodded. "Remind me to tackle her this afternoon while she's sober, or before she can get a chance to get a start."

He began at the top of the trunk and, taking out a

drawer at a time, dumped the contents on the table, handled each item thoughtfully and put it back. He ended with the shoe compartment under the hanger department, turning each shoe over and practically pulling the linings out. I watched him.

Next he took the cots apart, turning the mattresses, peering under the buttons, shaking the pad and sheets and heaping them on the floor. I made them up while he went through every garment hanging on the nails overhead.

There was a steamer trunk, belonging to Johnny, that was subjected to the same careful scrutiny. I couldn't decide whether any one thing interested him more than another. I rather thought not. I stood it as long as I could, but when he went back to the cartons of debris under the large picture window, I protested.

I said, "Have you any idea of what you are looking for?"

"Not the slightest," he replied, and tipped the first carton upside down on the floor. He dropped, cross-legged, beside the untidy heap and lighted a cigarette. He held the pack up to me companionably, and I sank to the easy chair beside him, after running a hand over it for wet paint. Someone had wiped it off, and the little that remained was well dried.

I stirred the stuff with a foot. "Why, as you asked before, would anyone destroy stinky old paint tubes? Johnny had enough money to buy others if they were jealous of his possessing them."

Max tipped his brown face up quickly, closing one eye to keep the smoke out. He squinted the other speculatively. He looked as if he were listening.

"Hey!" I said as a thought struck me.

Max took a cigarette out of his mouth and shadowboxed in my direction.

I said, "Did Ingram go through Iris Rutland's car?"

"Who is Iris Rutland?"

I tapped Max with a toe. "Johnny's wife, dope."

He thought a minute. "I think you've got something there, Abbie. He didn't say so."

I leaned back complacently and watched my neighbor poke around in the squeezed-out tubes of paint. He got nothing that I could see except a pair of dirty hands.

Presently I followed Max into the kitchen. He gave the contents of the cupboards the same painstaking going-over he had the stuff in the big room. There were few dishes, and less in the linen line, so it was soon over.

We moved to the storeroom. Max ignored the broken chairs, went through the commode there and the old sewing machine that didn't work, and found nothing of interest. He dropped to his haunches beside an untidy pile of boxes and cartons that the boys had brought some things in when they moved. He turned each one up and looked at the bottom and put it to one side.

I kicked a bundle toward Max. It was the plaster scrapings we had caught—was it only yesterday Ingram had probed for the bullet? Max tipped the coarse white dust into an empty box and smoothed out the paper.

I leaned over and read the address. To Mr. Edgar Pearson, care of, and so on. The wrapping from Bill's paints that Bill would never use.

I mentioned the waste of money.

Max said, "What do you mean, 'waste of money'? Bill took all those paints over to my house last night and dumped them in with mine."

"He did?"

"Yep. And now if I'm careful not to look, I can't tell

them from mine own. And so I can't be held morally responsible, can I?"

The two-way radio on the police car outside seemed to have taken on a new energy. It was positively bellowing. I heard Disbrow leave his perch on the steps and move over to the car.

I frowned at Max; I was puzzled. "What do you mean, 'morally responsible'?"

"Remember that I told you a Customs man couldn't bid in at an auction? And where did Bill get those paints?"

I understood. Well, if Bill wasn't going to use the paints, I was glad he had thought to give them to Max instead of leaving them there at the Blue Place to be utterly wasted the way Johnny's had been. I said, "When did he do all this?"

"After we got back with his car yesterday afternoon, remember?"

"I didn't see him take them over. Before or after you went to see Ingram?"

"Well! If it's anything to you—before."

I dropped the subject. If that was the way Max felt about a little neighborly curiosity! Perhaps I was a little put out. It isn't often that anything goes on between our two houses that I can't keep track of. I returned my gaze to the brown paper under Max's paint-smeared hands. I changed the subject.

"Who did send those paints, Max?"

Max consulted the return address. "Some bird with a six-digit number over in Germany. Can't make it out. The censor stamp—can't make that out either." Max peered closer. We were just too, too nice and polite to each other.

The two-way radio really was whooping it up outside! I raised my head and tried to make out what it was broadcasting. There was a pounding of footsteps on the porch, and Disbrow galloped across the kitchen to appear in the doorway, mouth open, eyes rolling in his white face.

"Johnson—Mr. Johnson."

Max lifted his head calmly. Damn him! He never showed excitement! He folded the wrapping paper before him carefully, maddeningly, as if it were important.

"Yes?"

Disbrow made a few squawking noises, tried again, and by swallowing diligently between words managed to get his message across. "Just came over the two-way—body in car—in gully back of Point—shot eight times—behind wheel—guy recently released from Army."

THIRTEEN

The gully behind the Point is closely related to the Point itself. In fact, the Point owes its very existence to the gully which was cut out of the hills by the action of an innocent-looking stream. That is, innocent-looking in the summer. In the spring the stream is a raging, roaring torrent, tearing the hills apart at the seams, spreading out at their base, and depositing a layer of silt on the Point. I don't know how many hundreds of years this has been going on, but in my lifetime I have seen the Point creeping slowly, but surely, out into the lake.

The farmers whose lands are separated by the gully have stopped fencing it in. Silly, when each spring flood carries the fence and posts down to the bottom of the lake! So the gully is open to the road and invitingly flat-looking at the entrance. Lovers innumerable have made car tracks there that have come to look like a road.

Only this car hadn't held lovers. I could easily understand why eight shots wouldn't have aroused the neighbors. So near the main road. So many backfiring cars operated by crazy kids after midnight. Even as far away as our cove they annoy us, waking us at all hours of the night.

Poor Frankie!

We, Max and I, were bouncing along at breakneck speed toward Harris Cove and the Point. My thoughts easily outstripped the car. I could see Frankie's none-too-intelligent face, his little blue eyes dancing with the love of living and that stark, staring fear I had watched quench that enthusiasm! That fear had had a solid, factual foundation! What had been the man's name?

Captain—Captain Gully? No—Glenn! That was it, Captain Glenn. What had he asked Frankie to call him? Ernie? Now I had it! Captain Ernest Glenn. I said it aloud and with considerable satisfaction.

"Captain Ernest Glenn."

Max took his foot off the accelerator. We bounded a little sidewise, like a shying horse, because the car controlled better under acceleration. He said crossly, "What!"

"Captain Ernest Glenn," I repeated. "He's the man who did it."

Max screwed his face into a puzzled mask. "Did what?"

"Shot Frankie eight times."

"Now I've heard everything!" Max turned his attention to his driving, manipulating a sharp turn and a steep drop as if it were an open road. "Now I've heard everything. Frankie who?"

"Frankie Sorbus."

"Oh!" said Max, and I was sure he didn't know what I was talking about. "What did you use, a crystal ball? Or were you there?"

I felt sad. He needn't be sarcastic. I said gently, "You

know I wasn't there. I was talking to Frankie Sorbus last night, and I heard Captain Ernest Glenn threaten him. He told him to forget the rank and call him Ernie."

"Oh!" said Max again. This time the sarcasm was doubly apparent. "He threatened him by telling him to call him Ernie. He should have said please!"

I ignored the quip. I said, "And he is a recently discharged soldier."

"Who is? Captain Glenn or your Frankie?"

"Why, Frankie! Or maybe the captain is too. I don't know. He was still wearing his uniform."

"And this Glenn——"

I interrupted, touching his arm. "Why, you know who Frankie is—you saw him that day at the auction! He had just gotten into town then. Remember, he rushed up and fell all over Orrin Keller?"

"All right, he threatened him. How? What did he say?" Max got back to the point of my story. We turned on to our own little road.

"I—well—it wasn't what he said——" I fumbled a little. "It was the manner in which he said it. That and the way the mere sight of this Glenn person scared Frankie. Green!"

Max closed his mouth in a grim line. His expression said I was touched. I didn't care! He'd find out when he got there! We drew up before the cottages; I got out and walked around the car.

The Johnson baby tumbled down the steps crying, "Daddy, Daddy, Daddy!" and made for the car.

Daddy waved, set the car in motion, and shouted for me to tell Mommie all and see that she had a good and adequate lunch, for he had had no breakfast. He'd be back shortly.

I took the baby's hand and turned her around. I said, "Never mind, darling. Daddy's busy. Where's Mommie?"

Mommie was taking a gingerbread out of the oven. "Did that rat drive away again?"

"Yes," I said. "But he will return, and hungry."

A sharp line appeared between Mommie's peaked brows. "Where've you been? What've you been doing?"

I said, "Come on over to our house, and then I can tell both you and Maggie and save repeating myself."

Mommie turned the oven off and hung her apron behind the door. She tucked her shirt into her slacks, hitching them up and tightening the belt around her small waist. She gave me a smile. "You'll have to repeat yourself, I'm afraid. Had you forgotten Bill's hospital trip?"

I had, completely. My face showed it.

Mommie laughed. "Dr. Custom ranted and raved a bit about your being gone—said something about you and Carrie Nation. So Grampie drove. Something about Dr. Custom having to leave early on account of calls. And Maggie might need help if they decided to release Bill right away."

I felt sick. "How"—I faltered—"how was Bill when he woke this morning?"

"Fine!" Mommie said. "Thought the hospital was a silly idea, but Dr. Custom insisted. Stay for lunch?"

"Sure," I said.

"Good. Now tell me all!"

I said I would and went to the bathroom to wash up. I felt as though I had been rolling in the road—grimy. Mommie lighted a cigarette, perched on the edge of the tub, and listened, with unconcealed interest, to my tale. I even went into my theories.

"Well," she said, "I'll not look for my girls till all the

excitement has died down on the Point. I sent them up for a carton of cigarettes. Hope they don't lose the money."

I set the table while she rummaged in the icebox. Mommie has the same aptitude for food concoction that Maggie has. By the time Max stopped in the driveway the table was inviting and Mommie was whipping cream for the gingerbread.

"Put on another plate," shouted Max as he swept through the house to the bathroom. "Hello, baby."

The baby tagged after him with her cry of joy, "Daddy, Daddy, Daddy!" She pushed the door open, not bothering to close it after herself. I wondered how Max got around that! But I didn't ask. By the time a man has fathered four girls he must have worked out some solution to the shared-bathroom puzzle.

I set another place.

Ingram arrived and was duly invited to use the most-used room in the house.

As we sat down to lunch Max leveled a long brown finger in my direction. "You were right, Abbie! Absolutely right. Only you had the wrong guys."

I opened my mouth. Max forestalled me. "It was Captain Ernest Glenn who was behind that wheel with eight bullet holes in his body."

"What!"

Max heaped his plate with potato salad and forked a slice of ham. "And Ingram tells me that your Frankie has left town."

Ingram salted his tomato slices. "Sometime in the night."

"But he won't get far," said Max. "Ingram has set the old wheels in motion, and he never misses."

Ingram turned his eyes in my direction. They were dull and mournful-looking, not at all like the snapping alert pair he had worn yesterday morning. He said slowly, and his voice matched his eyes, "I'm beginning to think I've missed on that other job. That Rutland shooting. Unless," he added, "they're tied up someway."

"Of course they're tied up!" stated Max. "You don't think two murders could happen in the same neighborhood in the space of two days and not be related."

Ingram thought about that. He shook his head finally. "To tell the truth, I've never had two murders within a month of each other. But that doesn't mean—I don't see any connection—yet."

Max laid down his eating implements in order to talk with his hands. "Look, Ingram. There's no other way to tackle these two." He spread the fingers of his left hand, ticking off the items he wished to emphasize with his right.

"What color is this what's-his-name's car?"

"Dark blue."

"What color is Bill Hunt's car?"

"Light blue."

"All right! Now—when we have dark blue paint on the left-hand side of Bill's car and light blue paint on the right-hand side of Glenn's car—what does it look like?"

"A sideswipe."

"But natch!" Max went back to eating in earnest, as though that ended the argument.

Mommie got up and opened another quart of beer and filled our glasses.

Max stopped chewing a piece of ham and stared at me, deep-set brown eyes piercing sharp under those lowered brows. I was frightened. I said, "What did I do now?"

He stared a moment longer, then resumed chewing. "Where have I heard that name, Ernest Glenn, Captain?"

"Why—I told you. This morning."

He drew his brows together again and shook his head. "No, before that. Think!"

"I can't," I wailed.

Ingram said, still puzzled, "But, Johnson, I don't follow! Where does a sideswipe tie up with yesterday's murder?"

"Mostly because it happened to Bill's friend. I don't know yet—but I will! I've got to use a little cerebration—that's all. That is, after I get everything you give me in the line of facts."

Ingram sighed tiredly. "You are welcome to any and all facts I possess. But I'm so doggone tired you'll have to dig for them."

Max looked out over the field before the porch and up to the hills. "You know," he said, "the fact that we have two murders to solve and one sideswipe makes it all the easier. A guy just couldn't keep on killing people and not leave a trail. And a new one each time—follow me? He's spreading himself too thin!"

Mommie gave the baby her dessert. She made short work of it and climbed down from her chair and leaned against her father sleepily. He rubbed her curly head. Mommie took her away for her nap.

I cleared the table, cut the gingerbread and served it. The men had lighted cigarettes in the interim, pushed their chairs away from the table slightly, and were smoking moodily.

Mommie returned. "I wish those girls would come home," she said. "They've been gone hours."

Max looked up sheepishly. "Sorry, wench. Your carton is in the car, and I gave the kids permission to stay with Nancy. They'll be home for dinner."

Mommie said, "Well!" She went out to the car, found

her cigarettes, came back to the table, and offered me one, pointedly.

Ingram blanked his cigarette. Mommie poured him a cup of coffee and he tasted his dessert. He said, "Better dig while I'm awake, Johnson."

Max said, his mind still far away, "That name! Still bothers me! Ernie Glenn!"

I looked down at my coffee cup. I couldn't help him, and I didn't like the feeling of being to blame.

Max said, hitching his chair closer to the table and resting both elbows on it, "All right—here we go. Give me— Captain Glenn's habits—friends—enemies—finances."

"Are you kidding?" Ingram shot up in his chair. He looked not the least bit sleepy. His thin, expressive face was alert, the black eyes snapping, sharp, and shiny again.

Max grinned. "On second thought—give me the setting first. Who found him, and stuff like that there."

Ingram relaxed. "Two boys were out hunting woodchucks. They came down the side of the gully—back— where you can't see from the road—and there it was.

"He had been shot eight times, all from the right and all close up so that he was blackened by powder, even burned. It's a wonder he didn't catch fire from so many."

Max interrupted, "Where do they get that eight-shots stuff?"

He frowned; his face cleared suddenly. "Don't tell me— I know. A forty-five Colt automatic—eight shots crosses off the possibility of a pistol—well—proves my first point."

Ingram nodded. "Tried to make a sieve of the poor jerk." He paused a moment, organized his thoughts, and continued: "Well, there is the car down in that dew-damp gully all night. It's low there and gets kind of cold. That made the outside of the car sweat at first, so that any fingerprints on the outside just rolled off like the sweat did.

"The doc hasn't got there yet, but from my experience it was done after midnight and before dawn.

" 'Cause the car cooled off, see? Then the old sun came up and climbed over the hill and hit the car. Warmed it up. You know how it would be. All closed. Not a window down. What happens? It sweats on the inside, of course. And that took care of any fingerprints."

Max nodded in agreement. Ingram went on.

"So the boys raced down to the Point and told the first fellow they ran into—Joe Turner, who was sweeping out his Arcade. Joe called the office, and the officer in charge gave it to me on the two-way."

We were silent for a space. Finally Max reached for the coffeepot and poured himself another cup. Ingram refused. Max said, "Go on. And I wasn't kidding about the habits —friends—enemies—finances."

Ingram groaned. He thought a minute. "Well——" he began. "No friends that we know of yet. His car is registered at Troy, New York. I've put through the usual to the police there. Naturally it's too soon——"

"I wonder where he was staying—if—at the lake?" said Max.

"He hasn't registered at a lake hotel," said Ingram. "I sent the usual, again, to the city hotels."

Max nodded.

"I presume," Ingram continued, "he's married. Wears a wedding ring. He also carries a gallery of glamour girls in his wallet, so—he may not be working at it."

Max held up a hand. "One of the girls wouldn't be Iris Rutland, would it? Or her blonde friend?"

Ingram thought a moment. "No." He tipped his head and shut his eyes. "I think I'd recognize either one of them. And I know I didn't run across either names—that I would recognize—Iris Rutland or—what was her name? Oh yes! Gladys DeLano."

Max groaned and grasped his head between both hands. "I should put you to work on my memory problem, Ernest Glenn!"

Ingram said, "I've enough to worry about."

Max lifted his head. "Finances?" he asked firmly, with the air of a man putting the impossible behind him and tackling the probable.

"He was carrying a bulging wallet filled with dirty bills. He had a bankbook that read four thousand."

Max whistled. "The game must have gone his way on the boat trip."

"The wallet was gone but the bankbook was left."

"How'd you know he was carrying so much?"

"Ed Vincent, at the bar at the hotel, saw it and told him he'd better keep it covered."

Max thought about the news. "Robbery, it looks like— but I'm thinking about the two others."

"What is it, then? You guess."

Max shook his head. "Who saw the victim last?"

I felt the blood rise to my face and pound uncomfortably in my neck. Max looked at me and waited. So I told Ingram about my encounter with the captain. I could see by their faces that merely getting Frankie Sorbus back was going to solve this murder as far as Max and Ingram were concerned. It made me mad! And at the same time that I was feeling impatient with the men facing me—a little doubt kept gnawing. I had always liked the kid Frankie. Yet, remembering his face, I wasn't too sure.

I ended my tale with, "If such a thing could be—that

Frank Sorbus did do this—it must have been self-defense, pure and simple."

Max guffawed and, putting a finger in Ingram's side—he sat on the right of Ingram—he a-a-a-a-a-a-a-ed. This threw Ingram into convulsions.

"Self-defense!" cried Max, tears in his eyes.

"Self-defense!" hooted Ingram. "With eight bullet holes in the dead body, fired from close up!"

Mommie patted my hand. I smiled at her, feeling awfully sorry for myself.

Max finally wiped his face with his napkin. He said, "That's all right, Abbie. I'd like you on my side when I do my first murder." He turned to Ingram. "I suppose you've put the boys onto questioning the neighbors—for sounds in the night and all that?"

"Yes."

"I can have that report, eh?"

"Of course."

"You searched the car?"

"You bet."

"Anything gone, been destroyed?"

"Nope."

"I meant to do one of those question-everyone jobs myself this morning—when the news came over the two-way up at the Blue Place. I planned on covering the farms between Marrowback and the cove."

"You can have my notes," offered Ingram.

"Thank you," said Max, and stood up. "I'm going to take a short nap. What about you?"

Ingram said, "Don't I wish I could! No. I've got to get back to the office and see what's come in. That's the penalty for being a professional." He left.

FOURTEEN

It was three o'clock before I awoke. I hadn't intended napping. I had gone home after helping Mommie with the lunch dishes and had gone upstairs. Bill's room drew me. I made the bed, which Maggie had merely opened to air. I felt like a heel not to have thought about her and Bill when I raced off this morning.

Too late now. I'd see that the house was straight, start the dinner, and do my best to show my sister I was sorry. I picked up Bill's pajamas and robe, hung them on the closet hooks, placed his slippers below, and closed the door. There were some handkerchiefs loose on the dresser top. I opened the drawer to replace them and was tempted. I looked for the gun.

It was gone! I looked everywhere and it stayed gone!

In my own room the bed invited. I would lie down for a few minutes until that sick feeling left, then I would go downstairs and see what was to be done. And it was three o'clock before I awoke. The phone was ringing.

Downstairs in the study, I lifted the receiver and said, "Hello," groggily.

"Abbie?" It was my sister Maggie.

"Yes."

"Well! Aren't you going to ask how he is?"

"I just—I haven't properly awakened yet, Maggie. What did they find?"

"Why don't you do your sleeping nights?" she said waspishly. That required no answer, and I gave it none. She waited an interval, then said, "Grampie and I should start home in an hour. We're to leave Bill here for one day at least. The X rays showed a concussion, but no danger."

"Good."

"They're so darn slow here, and Dr. Custom deserted us almost immediately. Some crazy phone call."

"Thank you," I said. "Have you any 'ruthers' for dinner tonight? I'm sorry I skipped out this morning. I meant to be back earlier."

Maggie cannot hold a grudge long. I felt her soften, over the wire. She sighed gustily. "Anything you wish. Look in the icebox. I did plan a chicken that Hungarian way— but I'm too upset to—— You must be too."

"I'll make out," I said. "Be careful."

We said good-by. I went back up the stairs, showered, and changed my clothes. I felt better.

I stepped out onto the porch. The lake was crowded with small craft; it boiled with holiday humanity; it hummed with merrymakers; it was hatefully typical of the Fourth. Only one ray of light on the dark subject: there were less and less of the noisemakers on the market for the celebrants to buy each year.

In the immediate foreground was my friend Max. He was making repeated trips from the house to the twenty-foot skiff tied to his dock.

Mommie and the baby were on the Lane porch. Virginia saw me and flew down her steps and hurled herself, panting, up mine.

"I heard the phone; any news?"

I told her.

"I meant to be over before they took him away, but Mother let me sleep and I never opened my eyes till almost two."

I said that she undoubtedly needed it: the sleep.

"I wonder," she said, "if I should call on him? Tonight?"

I didn't know, but I thought she could. Her face glowed.
I saw her looking at Mommie speculatively. Mommie was
stuck with Mrs. Lane, who is relentless when she gets a
neighbor into a porch rocker. I made a mental note to
avoid her till the trouble on our cove was finished and
done with. I waved to them and came down from my own
porch and crossed the lawn to Max. Virginia went on to
her house.

Max was adjusting the big old umbrella of Grampie's.
His arrangement was ingenious, to say the least: a neat
round hole in the seat, a broom handle in that, and, se-
curely lashed to the broom handle, the umbrella. The
broom handle's end was secured to the bottom of the
boat by four cleats, in the manner of a Christmas tree in a
soapbox.

His easel arrangement was equally ingenious. It looked
suspiciously like their collapsible metal invalid table: the
top part. It was likewise thrust down through a hole in
the seat and braced by cleats on the boat's bottom.

I said, pointing to the metal table, "What do you do
when that top swings out over the water?"

Max grinned up at me. "Those things keep me awake
nights. Mostly I keep it low enough to control it with my
knee. Have a good sleep?"

I nodded. Max climbed into the boat. I handed him a
cushion that lay on the dock, and he lifted himself far
enough off the hard board to slip it under. He certainly
looked silly. A couple of canvases were tipped against the
small seat in the fore part of the boat. On the bottom were
cigar boxes, each so full the lids wouldn't lie flat. A large
glass of assorted brushes set in the bottom of the boat, and
a few rags draped over the middle seat. I shook my head
and sat down on the dock, one leg under me, the other

hanging over the water. I said, "Want me to untie you?"

Max said, "I'm kind of waiting for those reports Ingram promised me. I suppose I could watch from the water and row in——"

I said, "I wondered if you were merely going to paint."

"I'm going to work on a canvas, but that doesn't keep me from thinking. Unless someone gets snoopy and watches."

I laughed. "The snooper wasn't born that you couldn't brush off! Here's your reports." A car had driven into the Johnson yard, and an officer was picking his way around the house. He was encountering several obstacles; obviously the baby had awakened from her nap and had been busy hauling out toys. He made it, handing Max a large manila envelope.

Max said, "Thanks a lot, Etter." Etter touched his forehead and turned his back on us and bravely faced the interceptions between himself and his car.

Max opened the envelope and took out a sheaf of papers. They were carbon copies. He riffled them over, and I said again, "Shall I untie you?"

Max said, "I don't mind going over these with you. I can talk to myself to you."

I said, "Geez! Thanks!"

"You're interested?"

I sobered instantly. "Indeed I am! I even have ideas."

"All right, then; shut up."

I shut up while he scanned the papers. Presently he spoke. "Reports on the people who live on the Marrowback Road." He stuck out his lips and made an impatient sound.

"Nothing; there never is! Some of them heard cars that they were sure were *the* one. Ask them what time and what makes them so sure, and they don't know from nothin'."

He put the papers into the envelope and shuffled them over once more. He selected one. "Report from the farms nearest the spot where Bill and Virginia were run off the road." He looked up and grinned at me. "Nearest isn't very near; you saw how far away that gas station is!

"Nothing of importance again. One woman thinks she heard screams." Max lifted his voice and called, "Ginnie!"

"Yes?"

"Did you scream last night?"

"No—I was too scared and it happened too fast."

He went back to the papers, discarding the one he had just read. "Ah! Report on Iris Rutland!" Max was pleased.

" 'Iris Rutland: waitress employed by the Metropolitan Restaurant in Royal, Texas. Resides at 166 Main Street in the Avalon Apartments. Married, husband in Pacific. Left Royal in company with Gladys DeLano, hostess employed at the same place and living in the same apartment. Traveled by car to New York, staying at the Dixie there for three days and then going to Woodstock, New York. At Woodstock the two women located the artists' colony known as "The Brush and Quill"—the colony is run for both artists and writers—and inquired for John Rutland. John Rutland had left a forwarding address which they obtained. They drove to Old Village, New York, and registered at the hotel on the Point at Ogg Lake. They arrived Monday, July first.' "

Max stopped reading. I said, "Go on."

"That's the end of the report. Here's a few pencil notes of Ingram's: 'Found letters in Iris Rutland's purse, from her husband, saying he was no longer interested in marriage and in marriage to her in particular. They were

very nasty letters. He says she can divorce him if she so
desires but that she cannot make him support her; he has
too much on her. He gives her explicit orders to leave him
alone. She can have the car and welcome, he has already
bought another.

"'Found loaded gun in Iris Rutland's car. Was about
to arrest her for the felony when she produced a permit.
Seems that she needed it in Royal. Carried large sums of
money at times.

"'She's driving me crazy asking for the body of her husband. She wants to start back for Texas—between you and
me, she's planning a duzy of a funeral—she and her side-
kick. They're also looking for a driving companion for
Gladys, who's going to drive back to Texas. Iris, the bereaved, will go on the train. Can't you just see her talking
about the baggage car ahead? In her cups? She has placed
John Rutland's car with the local dealer—probably sold by
now.'" Max folded this paper and placed it in the envelope.
He didn't laugh till he met my eye, then we both laughed.
"Mommie," he said, "told me all last night. I can see her,
can't you?"

I could and said so. Max selected another report.

"'Report on John Rutland: Released from Army, May
fifteenth, held rating of second lieutenant, went to Woodstock, New York, and signed up for the summer to study
there. Professional painting. He did some commercial art
before the war. Changed his mind about a summer at
Woodstock and signed out Tuesday, June twenty-fourth.
Forfeited his down payment of fifty dollars. Arrived at
Ogg Lake, Friday, June twenty-eighth. Was shot and
killed the night of July second.

"'John Rutland was insured for fifty thousand dollars
___'"

I said, "Hey!"

Max nodded. "I know—but he had had time to change the beneficiary; how was she to know——"

"Did he or didn't he?" I asked.

"It says here that his wife, Iris Martin Rutland, is the sole beneficiary. Now stop interrupting!"

"But, Max, there's your reason!"

Max put his tongue out and bit down on it. "You yourself said she was so drunk she couldn't navigate last night. Can you see her squeezing Virginia and Bill off the road and then luring the captain out to be shot to death in the gully?"

"But, Max, she could have pointed out Bill to the captain, gone with him while he ran them off the road, and then, drunk or sober, it isn't hard to shoot a man while he sits behind the steering wheel of his car."

"All right, tell me why!"

I couldn't. I sat and looked at the man before me. He had that faraway look in his deep-set, brow-shaded eyes again. He was thinking.

"Damn it all, Abbie! I can't help feeling that you're saying something sensible—but—it's like that name this morning that bothered me. Why? Why? Why?"

I said, "Go on."

" 'John Rutland,' " he read, " 'had an apartment in New York which he sublet. He had an income from some property in Pennsylvania, mining, and some shares in a large mail-order business in Pennsylvania also. Left by his parents.' "

He started to put the paper away. I said, "There's a note on the back." Max turned it over.

"Oh yes! More from Ingram. 'Gun missing. We know there was one because the mark is plain in the top drawer of the trunk and' "—here Max looked over the top of the paper, comically, like a heavy-browed monkey peeking out of a barrel—" 'the permit to carry same is in Rutland's wallet.' "

I said, "Yaa."

Max said, "So what?"

"He did have one."

"Still, so what?"

"Find it! It's the one."

"Still——"

I chorused, "So what!"

Max put the paper away and selected another. "Frank Sorbus," he announced. My heart pinched.

" 'An Old Village boy; both parents dead, one married sister living in city; unmarried. Released from Army and arrived in city on July first. Stayed with sister one day. Got old job back with Keller Jewelry—handy man—really employed by Orrin Keller. Has rooms over garage on Keller property on Ogg Lake.

" 'On the night of July third went with party to dance at the Point at Ogg Lake. Escorted Miss Clarabelle Connors from Old Village. Left the party a little after ten and didn't join them again until around eleven. Had words with Miss Connors; she objected to his drinking, and that seems to be what he left the party for. She claims he was drunk when he rejoined her. Miss Connors insisted on his taking her home, which he did, leaving her at the door immediately. He did not try to explain his conduct; rather he seemed to be relieved to get rid of her, according to Miss Connors.

" 'Sometime between ten and eleven Frank Sorbus was seen, first at a table near the dance hall, when he ordered a drink in company with Miss Alberta Harris, and later at the bar, when he tripped over a couple in company with an army officer who flashed a wallet of money. The waiter at the table was Edward Lang, and the man at the bar was Edward Vincent.' "

I held up a hand. "You're getting tiresome, my friend. You're making up a lot of junk."

"Oh, I am, am I?" Max thrust the paper under my nose, much too close for reading. I pushed it away.

"How do you like having your name bruited about with those of well-known criminals?"

"Max," I cried, "he isn't, believe me! He's just a poor, dumb kid I had in eighth grade, and I won't let you——"

"What?"

"Well—you know what I mean. You've got to work from the premise that he didn't do it."

"He's just as good a suspect as your dame, Iris!"

"No!"

"Well, let me finish. Where was I?" Max mumbled and muttered until he caught up with himself. " 'At nine-thirty this morning Orrin Keller, Ogg Lake, reported Frank Sorbus missing, along with the 'thirty-eight Ford sedan he had turned over to Sorbus to use. We have broadcasted the description of the car along with the license number and have asked the city police to call on the sister. No report yet.' "

Max folded the paper and put it in with its fellows. He said nothing, and I kept silent. But my thoughts raced. Nothing in that report about Tuesday night; where had Frank Sorbus been that evening? And again, every return-ing soldier boy seemed to be keeping his gun. Where was Frankie's?

Finally I said, I had to know, "No gun?"

Max fished the paper out once more. "Sorry, Abbie. I purposely left it out, you seemed so——"

I smiled. "Stubborn? I am!"

Max read, " 'Sorbus owns gun, probably his army forty-five. Has neglected to register it. Must have weapon with him, as it is not on premises over garage.' " Max put it away again.

I said, "Thank you." I moved my leg out from under me; it was asleep. I asked, "That all?"

Max smiled. "No. Here's one on Bill. Want to hear it? And oh yes! Ingram has called in the boys from the Blue Place."

I wrinkled my nose. "I know all about Bill, never mind."

Max leaned forward in the boat. "You know, Abbie, he and Virginia could have faked that accident."

"What in the world for?" I asked.

"Well . . ." he pondered. I waited, getting a little cross. That idea was a little farfetched. He stuck to it, though. "Suppose," he said, "let's suppose that Bill did go back to the Blue Place on Tuesday night and they got to fighting. Over Virginia, of course. Bill confesses to her and she is sympathetic, naturally. That kind of battle—male against male for a female—is as old as the world and has never made a woman too darn mad yet. Flatters her no end."

"And . . . ?" I said, and I tried to make it sound sarcastic. I failed miserably; I sounded scared.

"They go for this moonlight ridge. Were you there last night when they made up? No, you were drinking the boys under the table."

I made an unladylike sound. Max grinned.

"It was very funny. She and Mommie walked into the bar, looking harassed. I know now—they were being heckled by those Texas dames—but I didn't then, and I wondered what was the matter! No poise, you know! And Bill had just been telling me how Virginia had given him

the brush-off before dinner and how he was going to re-
enlist and maybe end up in Mongolia and be a lama—you
spell it with one *l*. I just got through telling him he could
be a llama with two *l*s easier than that: get married. I've
been a beast of burden for how long? It doesn't matter.

"Well, in they walk, looking as if they had been pinched
you-know-where as they came through the door. They look
wildly around the room, spy us, and make for us like a
couple of bees hitting for home with the pollen and loaded.
I think Mommie is going to throw her arms around me and
I prepare to defend myself, and then I get a look at Bill!

"Virginia smiles at him—one of those radiant smiles
that are as false as your mother-in-law's teeth—and the
poor guy is yammering and yawping like I've never seen
before outside of those people who shake the bars on the
big red building where the paper-doll-cutting contests are
held.

"So I prepare to defend Bill, instead of myself; his
danger is greater, he is young, while I've left my youth behind me. Too late! Too, too late. Bill's a goner, but good,
and what's the Army's loss is posterity's gain."

I shifted uneasily. I said, "Go back to your case against
Bill and Virginia."

"Just that they could have faked the accident."

"But why?"

"To make it look as though the same person is after Bill
who was after Rutland."

"And the other fellow, the captain?"

Max thought about it. "They wouldn't want the money.
It could be an entirely different case if the captain could
have been a friend of Rutland's and accuse Bill."

"You've got to have seen them together. You can't just
accuse Bill without having seen them together."

Max hunched forward once more and rested his chin on the knuckles of his right hand. "I know," he said. "That's the weak link." We were silent for a considerable time.

I said finally, "You get on with your thinking. I don't want to hold you up. How do you go about it? Thinking, that is."

Max kept his chin down, lifted his brows, and looked out from under them at me. "Mostly," he said, "I try them on for size—like I just did with the idea of Bill being the one. Work it out to the end, and then discard it if it doesn't fit.

"Today I think I'll begin at the beginning, like this: Unless Johnny was killed for hate, he was killed because the killer was looking for something.

"Unless Bill was hit over the head for hate, he was hit over the head for—because the hitter was looking for something.

"Unless the captain was killed for hate—no—that doesn't fit." Max screwed his face up, eyes shut, nose wrinkled, brows drawn together, mouth tight. I watched him, wishing I could get into that head of his and watch it work. He opened his eyes, dropped his brows, smoothed his nose, and straightened in the seat. He picked up the oars and smiled at me.

"What I mean is that today I'll work from the victims and the possible whys, instead of my usual manner of working from the murderers and the possible motive, means, and opportunity."

I pulled the rope out of the ring on the dock and tossed the end into the boat. I said, "If the murderer didn't hate the murderee, what in heck was he looking for in such varied and different places?"

Max rowed away.

FIFTEEN

I looked at my watch. Four o'clock; Maggie and Grampie should be starting for home by now. I waved in the direction of the Lane porch and walked firmly toward my own. No one was going to lure me into the neighborhood of Mrs. Lane, and I was pretty sure she wouldn't seek me; there had been a definite coolness between the Lanes and the Harrises—excepting Virginia—since Dr. Custom had made the remark: "I'd always heard about the long lane that had no turning, and it's a damn lie. This Lane isn't long, she's short and fat, and I'd defy anyone to turn her— off!" Dr. Custom's voice carries well—too well—and Mrs. Lane, who had left our porch, changed her mind and had started back in time to hear it. I'm afraid she heard our dutiful laughter also. Maggie and I have learned to laugh at Dr. Custom's jokes immediately; otherwise he repeats them.

Orrin Keller was fastening his beautiful electric boat to our dock. My goodness, did the man have a crush on me? Seemed to me I was seeing a lot of Orrin this summer! I put a smile on my face and waited at the steps.

Orrin raised up from his task, stood still a moment, drew a deep, weary breath, and braced his shoulders. He sagged again, as though the result wasn't worth the effort required. He plodded toward me, no smile on his large, close-shaven face that was usually a nice healthy pink. It wasn't pink this afternoon, it was gray, and what had been firm, hard, fat cheeks had drooped into dewlaps on either side of the down-drawn, disappointed mouth.

I kept the smile on my face. As he drew nearer he pulled the corners of his mouth up faintly. He stopped in front of me, and he didn't seem nearly as big a man as I had thought him to be.

"Good afternoon, Alberta."

"Hello," I said.

"Had to get away from that place of ours. Jeannette has it overrun—everybody squawking and screaming around —can't stand it! Thought it might be quiet here. Thought you and Maggie wouldn't mind if I came around."

I opened the screen and invited him in. "Come on up on the porch; I'll buy you a drink."

He sank to the glider, made a satisfied sound, and crossed his legs comfortably. I went out to the kitchen, got a bottle of rye, two small glasses, and two glasses of water. I put them on a tray, carried it to the porch, and set it on the table near the glider and said, "Help yourself. You look as if you could use a drink."

"I can." Orrin's voice always suggested a whisper without actually being one. It isn't a hoarse voice; rather it's a light one, keyed to a pitch that carries as far as the listener and no farther. It always interested me; I was constantly trying to figure out how he achieved the effect. Perhaps it came from years of talking across the counter to customers. Perhaps the knack was one that storekeepers were born with, a sort of occupational aptitude.

Orrin poured two whiskys, passed me one, and tasted his. He set the glass back.

"I've just had a shock—knocked me for a—— Well!"

"I know," I said sympathetically.

Orrin's light blue eyes sharpened, searching mine. "You do?"

"Yes, if you mean Frank Sorbus."

He shook his head sadly. "After all I did—I treated that fellow like a son——" He put his hands palms together in front of his paunch and pressed the two wrists against himself hard. "There must be some explanation! Some other—— I won't—I refuse to condemn the boy till I see him." He closed his eyes tiredly. "It has been a shock."

"Do you want to talk about it?" I asked.

"No, I'd rather not; it hurts." But I knew he was kidding himself. He was dying to tell me all about it. It would be a relief, rather than a painful experience. The painful part was behind him.

I deliberately fed him the proper questions.

"When did you first suspect?"

"I didn't, Abbie. Not till this morning, when the car was missing. Then I can't say I really suspected him of anything more than the theft of my car. It was just now, when I got the news broadcast, that I felt the full impact of the man's deceit."

"Broadcast? I'm sorry, we haven't had our radio on."

"They've found the car."

I said nothing, wondering if the churning in my stomach showed in my face. Orrin took out a handkerchief and mopped his forehead. He was sweating, and yet the face before me stayed gray.

He lowered his voice; that voice is never loud anyway. "They have found a gun and a wallet of money. The gun was in the glove compartment, locked, and the money under the seat stuck up into the springs."

"Where," I asked, "did they find the car—how?"

"In the city. It was backed up against the wall in that parking lot near the Federal Building. I suppose he backed it up thinking no one would see the license plate. The Federal Building is closed over the week end, and I suppose he'll come out of wherever he's hiding and expect to drive away in it. That is——" Orrin faltered. "They'll catch him then."

"Don't feel so badly," I said. "If he did those terrible things, he's guilty and deserves——"

"Ah, Abbie, put yourself in my place. Think of how you feel about your nephew! You must have had some anxious moments when his friend was found——"

"I did. I know what you mean." And I did, too.

"I regret reporting the car. I'll never forgive myself. If Frank Sorbus had some secret, special grudge to settle with that captain—— Who knows—who knows what went on over there in Europe?"

"He couldn't have had any secret, special grudge against Bill's friend," I said. "He was over there in the Pacific!" I spoke a little sharply; let's keep this conversation logical.

Orrin smiled placatingly. He started to reach out with his hand to pat mine, realized I was sitting out of reach, and drew back. He bobbed his head up and down. "You're so right, dear girl. I hadn't thought of that. And, too, he shouldn't have taken the money. The police report said there was seven hundred dollars in that wallet."

I felt the palms of my hands ooze wet. This was awful! A woman should feel one way or another about such a person as Frank Sorbus. If he was guilty, I should hate him and be glad when the police caught him. I shouldn't have this feeling that, whatever he had done, he was, somehow, not to blame for his own actions. I could see his sharp face, his not-bright face, his nice, homely, wouldn't-hurt-a-flea face, and I didn't want the police to find him. I wiped my hands on my handkerchief.

Orrin finished his whisky, savoring it. I said, "Please have another; you can't——"

"Fly on one wing?" Orrin finished the platitude for me.

I had been going to say, "Walk on one leg." Same difference! He filled his glass again.

Orrin shifted on the glider; it protested, squeaking. He said, "Where is that nephew of yours? Out painting a landscape?"

I sat up straight. Didn't everyone know? I said, "Didn't you know? He's in the hospital."

"Hospital!" It was Orrin's turn to sit up straight. He reached for his drink and threw it down his throat. "Hospital!" he repeated. "Why didn't you tell me?"

I told him. I had an interested audience. And I could almost see the thoughts forming in his mind behind those blue eyes of his, thoughts about poor Frank Sorbus. Though how he was going to connect Bill with Frankie, I wasn't able to imagine.

I slumped back in my rocker, moving it slightly, rocking; the motion comforted me. To make conversation I said, "I suppose finding the car—could that be why Ingram called off the boys up at Blue Place?"

Orrin settled back against the glider cushions and clucked his tongue. "And I thought you were going to have a nice little artists' colony here in Harris Cove."

I smiled wryly. "One got shot; one gave it up. Just Max left." I lifted my head, indicating Max in the skiff under his silly umbrella, bobbing around in the water. I would have given a pretty to have seen him work with brush and canvas on that holiday lake. The powerboats kept it churned up like a college swimming pool on an annual meet.

Orrin said, "One gave up? Your nephew?"

I nodded. "Dumped all his paints in with Max's and said, 'The heck with it.'"

"Whatever did he do that for?"

"Decided he wasn't the artistic type!"

"Well, I never! Those paints represent an outlay of money. He should have thought before he invested." The thrifty merchant was speaking now.

"They didn't cost much. And Max will be able to use them," I explained.

"Well, I should think he would!"

Now what in the world made Orrin use that indignant tone? What was it to him? Bill had a perfect right to give away anything he wanted, hadn't he? I began to understand: the typical storekeeper's attitude again—anything unused and saleable should be sold—not given away. I smiled at Orrin.

"Look," I said, waving an arm in the direction of Max. "Look at how happy the man is! He and Bill's paints."

Orrin got up and stepped to the screen, the better to see Max. He made an unconvinced noise, a grunt. "Don't tell me that the man's trying to paint a picture out there on the lake!"

"Nothing else but," I said.

"He's crazy!"

I said, "Right."

Orrin came back to the glider and sat down and poured himself another drink.

The phone in Papa's study rang. A long ring. I got up and went through the doorway and took the receiver off the hook. It was Frankie Sorbus.

I recognized the voice—a miracle of acumen, for if Frankie had been frightened last night, today he was terrified. Terrified beyond all human sound. His voice was animal-like, quacky, like Donald Duck. High, metallic, it vibrated the diaphragm in the receiver unpleasantly.

I said the usual, "Hello."

Silence while he tried to recognize my voice. Then that appalling cacophony. "Miss Harris!" I could almost see him raise and lower his eyebrows.

I opened my mouth to say "Frankie"; he anticipated it a fraction of a second before I got it out and screamed, "No! Don't say it. Don't say anything unless I tell you to!"

I closed my mouth and held the receiver away from my ear. I waited. My ear hurt.

I could sense, over the space between, the panic that took hold of the man. I could see him shy away from the instrument, approach it once more, sidling, on the bias. When he spoke this time it was a croak, a whispered caterwaul. "Are you still there? Say 'Yes.'"

I said, "Yes," and for the life of me couldn't help the backward apprehensive look that I cast in the direction of the door to the porch. Orrin was looking my way, a frown between his light brows, his head tipped to one side. We dropped our eyes, both of us, embarrassed to be caught watching each other.

Frankie was talking. "I didn't know who to call, Miss Harris. I thought of you; you were always nice to me. Are you there? Say 'Yes.'"

I repeated, "Yes."

"I thought you could help me, maybe. Are you alone?"

"No."

"Be careful!" Frankie was shrieking again.

"Yes."

"Could you talk to that neighbor of yours? That Johnson? He's a right guy, isn't he?"

"Yes."

"I'm hiding now. I've been framed—I can't tell you now; I wouldn't dare to over the phone."

"Yes," I said, it seemed a nice safe word. And it seemed to keep him satisfied.

"I've been framed, Miss Harris. And I didn't know for sure till I heard the broadcast a while ago. I've been framed awful."

"Yes."

"You don't think I did it, do you?"

Surprisingly enough, I didn't. I searched my mind, my true thoughts, and was astonished. Frankie touched me somewhere. Frankie's need was so terrible that I couldn't have refused to help him had I any doubts. And I hadn't. I said, "No."

"I didn't. But I know who did, and I haven't a Chinaman's chance of being believed on my own. Someone'll have to help me."

"Yes."

"I'm hiding. It won't be for long, 'cause I know I've been framed and I'll have to move."

Frankie seemed a bit hysterical. Like the man lost in the woods. He was getting back to where he started. I risked a soft, "Where are you now?"

That brought a piercing shriek once more.

"Don't talk! Jeez—Chri—don't talk."

There was an exclamation from the porch and the sound of breaking glass. Orrin appeared at the doorway, holding one hand with the other and making a face. He opened the hand to show blood running from a cut palm and said, with silent lips, "Lavatory?"

I put my hand over the mouthpiece and indicated the lavatory door to my right. Orrin went in, and I could hear him running water.

Frankie must have sensed another presence in the room,

for he said, low and hoarse, "Who's there?" Then quickly, before I could answer, "No! Don't say it."

I kept still.

There was an odd sound over the wire now. A sound as if the man were crying. May well have been. He controlled himself; spoke again after a small space.

"I'll have to get to your place. There's no other way. After dark. Or could you meet me?"

"Yes."

"Where? I wish I could think! I'm too scared."

"Here?"

"Too many people."

I whispered, "Marrowback?"

"You mean the place—where——"

"Yes."

"Isn't it lousy with police?"

"No."

"Were they called off?"

"Yes."

"I'll be there. Right after it's dark."

"Yes."

"Oh God!" It was a prayer. I waited.

"Oh God! I can't. I haven't the nerve to show my face— I'm afraid."

"Where, then?" I asked. The pause this time dragged so that I thought he had gone away, letting the receiver dangle.

"Could you come as far as the city line?" he asked finally. "Could you?"

"Yes." I didn't hesitate. "City line."

"After it's good and dark."

"Yes," I said, reassuring him, "dark."

"What kind of a car do you drive?"

I had to think. I said, "Mine is a 'thirty-eight Ford."

"Drive around the first block—I'll be watching from somewhere and hail——" There was a click and the line went dead.

I hung up the receiver and tried to arrange my face. Orrin came out of the lavatory still holding his hand.

I said, "I'll get a bandage."

"So clumsy of me!"

I dressed his cut and led the way outdoors once more and pondered what we'd talk about now. I was saved the trouble; people began to arrive. Grampie drove in. Max rowed in from the lake and tied his craft up to the dock. Mommie and Virginia walked over the grass from the Lanes' to the Johnsons' dock to greet Max. He had closed his umbrella, climbed up on the dock, and, grasping the rusty, baggy thing somewhere in the middle, brandished it like the lad in the poem by Longfellow who cried, "Excelsior!"

Grampie and Maggie came around the house, and Orrin and I stepped down from our porch. The talk was general.

Orrin displayed his hand and described his clumsy accident. "Don't know what in the world made me drop the glass, and then, dropping the glass, what in the name of common sense made me dive for it the way I did! Like to have bled to death if Florence Nightingale hadn't been there with her little old bandage." Chuckling and expecting everyone else to think it was amusing.

I wondered if, when I bandaged his hand, the man thought my hands were trembling at the sight of blood. And, surprisingly, I found I was trembling less and less as I realized no one was paying any attention to me. Each person was interested in himself.

Max's eyes glittered like jet. The exuberance, the gloating, the jubilation vibrated over and over his face like an aurora borealis. Mommie saw it, and the reflection was in her eyes, warm, blue green, joyous.

Mrs. Lane prattled.

"That silly girl of mine wants to go in to the hospital to-night. With all this traffic! And she's talked Mommie into going with her, Grampie."

"Fine."

Maggie said, "Visiting hours are from seven to eight-thirty."

Virginia threw her mother an impatient look and stepped out on the dock. "Can we see what you were do-ing, Max?"

"Sure! Go ahead; I'm not proud." Max waved the um-brella in a generous gesture.

We moved dockward, everyone talking at once, as peo-ple do when something is to be displayed.

I asked Maggie how things had gone at the hospital to-day. Grampie was explaining to Mrs. Lane the intricacies of X ray. Mrs. Lane was bobbing her head and talking about her operation. The baby, both arms around her father's leg, was impeding his walking. Orrin Keller was expounding his theories of the germ-killing properties of the various antiseptics on the market to Mommie, who wanted noth-ing so much as she wanted to push him off the dock so that she could get her husband alone and find out what had switched on that neon effect in his face. I could read her impulse because she was too, too nice to Orrin; her manner verged on the gushy.

I held back, letting Maggie pass me.

Max pried the little arms apart and detached his daugh-ter from his person.

I said, "So?"

Max made a single downward gesture. "I've got it!"

"No!"

"Figured it out not ten minutes ago."

"Can't you tell us?"

"Had the answer right in the boat with me—no—can't tell you yet—got to get up to the Blue Place for verification."

I stared out at the boat. I said, "What do you mean—answer in the boat with you? All I can—all you have there—are your oils."

"So?"

"And Bill's."

"Go to the head," Max said, and stuck the long ferrule of the umbrella into a crack in the boards and leaned on it, grinning.

"Yoo-hoo!" There was a musical trill from our lawn. Around the house, our house, tripped Johnny's wife and her blonde companion. I gave them an openmouthed stare and stood still, waiting.

Iris Rutland was a lady today. Her face wore a haughty expression of the manner-born and the flush of a pretty good start for the afternoon. Her eyes were unfocused and her walk not too steady, but she was a lady. She was wearing a sheer black dress with white accents. Her friend wore pink.

She shook my hand daintily, leaning a little forward and breathing into my face. I staggered back.

"You must be Alberta Harris!" My gosh! Was she going to pretend we had never met? "I'm Iris Rutland, Johnny's wife. I felt I couldn't leave without stopping by and thanking you and your sister—— This is your sister Margaret, isn't it?" Yes, she was.

Iris Rutland drifted past me, reached Mrs. Lane, and

started through the same ritual with her. We put her right, but it took some doing! Virginia and Mommie looked scared, edging a bit toward shore.

Iris Rutland finally accepted Maggie. "So you're Margaret Harris!" She seized Maggie's hand, lifted it daintily, and breathed on her. Maggie backed up hastily. Iris swept out on the dock's end, recovered herself in the nick of time from stepping off, and returned halfway.

She waved airily. "This, folks, is my very dear friend, Gladys DeLano; Gladys, Miss Harris. Or should I say Misses Harris?" She tinkled laughter, eying the men for approval.

Gladys DeLano, heavy-hipped, thick-ankled, a little unsteady on her feet, followed her leader and struck a ladylike pose, one hand on her hip, the other behind the pink gardenias in her golden hair. "I'm so glad to meet you. I've heard so much about you."

Maggie and I exchanged a surprised look. I heard Maggie say, "What!" I moved out on the dock too.

"Oh! Oh!" Iris caught sight of the easel thrust through the seat in Max's skiff. "Gladys! A painter! Just like Johnny!" Iris spun around, arms thrown out dramatically, making soft little cries, closing her eyes, then fluttering them as if to blink back the tears. She dropped to the dock gracefully, if a bit unsteadily, picked up the canvas from the improvised easel and, holding it at arm's length, gazed at it as if it were a landscape by Cox or Constable. As it happened to be a rather dull background, with nothing of interest in it, the audience on the dock was a bit wonder-eyed. In picking up the canvas, Iris relinquished her purse, an oversized white job that opened and spilled its contents as it hit the bottom of the boat. A handkerchief fluttered down and drifted over the jelly glass of brushes like a small parachute. The bag would be white no longer. It lay on an open cigar box that I happened to know held some of the smeariest paint tubes in existence.

Gladys dutifully came over to her bereaved friend and bent to the boards beside her, with a large, muscular arm around her shoulders. "Take it easy, sister. This ain't going to bring him back." The husky alto was all tremolo.

The congregation on the dock began to back toward shore. Horror on some faces, disgust on others. I began to wish someone would do something.

The blonde shifted her hold on her friend and lost her purse. It followed Iris's to the floor of Max's boat, splattering miscellanea. They'd never get the respective contents sorted out.

Someone decided to do something.

Orrin jumped into the awkward breach. He said brightly, "Well, I've got to be going." He walked across the lawns, untied his boat, and glided silently around the end of our dock. He drew up beside Max's skiff.

Our two visitors were impressed. Trance-like, Iris laid the picture down, and they both watched Orrin with avid, appreciative eyes. I didn't blame them; Orrin's craft always hits strangers right there, between the eyes. Red leather upholstery would be speaking their language. Like an automaton, Iris floated to her feet. Gladys followed.

Orrin said, "I have to stop at the hotel. Perhaps you ladies would do me the honors?"

And here is where Orrin made his mistake. He should have pulled up on the other side of the dock. Or, better still, he should have gone on about his business and not played the gentleman. I thought the two women would knock each other down getting to Orrin.

They both accepted with shrill voices and ladylike grace,

scrambling, one after the other, into Max's boat as the shortest distance between two points—the dock and Orrin's boat. I watched with horrified fascination. Each stopped long enough in the smaller boat to retrieve her purse, stuffing things pell-mell into her pouch, bleating all the time, soprano and alto. Then scrambling from one boat to the other, with a display of stocking tops, garters, and white thighs.

Orrin, holding onto both boats, helped them as best he could. Leaning over as he was, he had a little trouble with his paunch, which seemed to be in the way. I suppose that's why Gladys fell in.

Iris Rutland made the exchange first; she was the thinner and quicker of the two. She settled herself against the red leather cushions, preening herself, thinking her black dress looked well against the crimson, regarding her companion complacently; she wouldn't look so well against red.

Iris jumped up with a soft squeal; some object was missing from her purse.

Orrin, leaning way over into Max's boat, punctiliously helping Gladys, was thrown off balance, and it was done! A deep alto cry, a splash followed by a soliloquy of invectives such as has never been my fortune to hear before. I learned three new words.

SIXTEEN

We watched Orrin's boat out of sight with unconcealed relief. He rounded the Point and disappeared. I could imagine the entrance they made, past the sitters on the hotel porch!

Mommie, the last minute, decided against going to the hospital with Virginia. I was about to say I'd go—one easy and natural way to pick up Frankie would be just to run across him casually at the city line at dark. Then Mrs. Lane spoiled it all by deciding she had a friend in the hospital, at least she thought she was there, and even if she wasn't, there was bound to be someone she could call on!

Anyway, I hadn't told Max about Frankie's call.

Grampie went into the Johnson house and Maggie departed for ours, leaving Max and Mommie and me. Max leaned against that silly umbrella, regarding us with knit brows.

Mommie said, "I got one look at Max, and wild horses couldn't drag me away; something's going to happen."

"What?" I asked.

We both stared at Max. He stopped leaning against the umbrella, picked it up by its bulky middle, and said, "I'm going to use your phone."

Mommie put both hands on her hips and stuck out her red lower lip and watched him into our house. She said, "I positively hate him when he gets like that."

I thought about Frankie. I said, "Like what?"

"Smug and sure of himself and at the same time facetious. Which all means that he's scared to death inside and wishing he was doing anything else in the world. It means he hates himself, so he makes himself obnoxious as he knows how, hoping people will be unpleasant to him. Like those religious fanatics in the old days who beat each other up and down the road."

Max stuck his head out the study door. "They beat each other up and down the back."

"See what I mean?" Mommie's eyes were too bright, too near tears.

I took her hand and pulled her toward the porch. We sat on the glider in time to hear Max give Ingram's number.

"Johnson speaking. Ingram there? . . . Home? . . . Got the number handy? . . . 205R—thanks."

He hung up and called 205R. "Ingram? Good—I caught you—Johnson. Anything new?"

There was a pause while the phone crackled with Ingram's crisp voice.

Max said, "Sounds reasonable. I'll be over. I'm going to the Blue Place for something—this is it, all right."

There were more crackles, more sputtering.

"Not over the phone," said Max. "I'll see you very soon. If what I want is at the Blue Place, it won't take long—— No, I don't know how, but we'll find a way. . . . Good-by."

Now was the time to tell him about Frankie.

Max came out on the porch carrying the umbrella. Mommie and I pretended not to notice it. I heard Mommie mutter, "Exhibitionist."

I said, "Tell us how and who."

"Sorry, girls, I've got to get going."

Mommie said, "Not until you tell us!"

"What do you want to know?"

"What went through your head out there on the lake! How you arrived at whatever you arrived at and are you there yet?"

Max swung a straight chair around, straddled it, and hooked the umbrella over the back. He took out a pack of cigarettes, selected one and lighted it. "I'll give you about five minutes of my valuable time, good people. Ingram is going to eat now." He smoked a moment, put his head down on his hands, clasped one over the other on the chair back. Smoke drifted up from the cigarette between his fingers. He raised his head. "This is the way it went, if I can remember.

"I told you how I figured that if the two who were killed weren't killed for just plain hate, they were put out of the way for something they possessed.

"And it stands to reason that if the killer had found what he was looking for at the Blue Place he wouldn't go around pushing people off the road and then belting them over the head and then go through their car. So . . .

"What was in the Blue Place before the night of July second and wasn't there on that night?

"Clothes? Money? Papers of any sort? It had to be something small to be in the places the marauder looked. What?

"What was taken away in the evening that had been there in the daytime?

"Then what had been in Bill's car on the night of July second and not in Bill's car on the night of July third?

"I thought and thought. Then I decided to quit thinking and pretend to paint, and then I had it! Bill's new paints that he had given me! And don't ask me why that other poor guy was shot last night. I don't know, but I will as soon as I verify what I think I saw on the wrapping paper that Bill's paints came in."

"That's why you're going——"

"Right."

Mommie said, "But will that tell you who?"

"I hope so! I hardly think I need it—but on the other hand, I'm going to get up there and get it before the other guy does."

I cleared my throat. "Max—I had a——"

Max interrupted me. "Here's another point—where did the paints come from? Europe! . . . Where did Frankie

come from? Europe! . . . Where did the captain who was
killed come from? . . . Right again!"

Maybe I didn't want to tell Max about Frankie! I said,
"So you have your mind made up that it was Frankie
Sorbus?"

"Not made up, Abbie; rather say, open to the sugges-
tion."

Mommie said, "What value could the paints have—
that a man could be killed for them?"

"I don't know yet—but I'm going to find out."

"How?"

"Ingram does *some* work, you know! Ingram has a well-
disciplined, well-trained staff who are on the job and
whose business it is to look into these tiresome details—
like where were you on the night of July third and at what
time?"

Mommie said, and her voice was low and thin and
scared, "Stop kidding with us and get on about your business and get it over with."

Max stood up, lifted his umbrella from the chair back,
and wheeled to the door. Mommie whispered, "Dear God!
Be careful!" He left.

Maggie came downstairs, and I heard her go to the
kitchen. My conscience smote me, and I got up to help
her.

"That rat left me with the boat to clean out," Mommie
said. Her voice rang with false cheerfulness. She went
down the steps and out to the dock, where she lifted up
the canvas and went into the house, presumably to place it
on the plate rail.

I said to my sister, "Let's just make a couple of sand-
wiches, shall we?"

Maggie said she wasn't really hungry. I knew I would have trouble eating anything; I still had Frankie on my conscience.

Mommie came back up on the porch with a puzzled expression on her face and the three cigar boxes in her hands.

I said, "What's the matter?"

She said nothing but opened the top box and tipped it so I could see. It was empty!

I grabbed it out of her hand, and she opened the second. The same! And the third!

I said, "What does it mean?"

"They were full when he went out on the lake."

I thought a space. "Those two women!" I shouted it so that it brought Maggie out on the porch.

Mommie and I stared at each other. I could see those two supposedly drunken women flopping around in Max's boat. I could see them scattering the contents of their large purses on the floor boards, and I could plainly see them scrambling around trying to pick up. They couldn't possibly have made the mistake of putting Max's paint tubes in. If they did, it was no mistake! And there was more than Max's paint in those cigar boxes! Mommie, I could see, had the same thoughts.

I said, "Shall we go up to the Blue Place and tell him?"

"He ought to know!"

Maggie said, "Know what?"

Mommie said, "Someone has stolen Max's paints."

"Whatever for?"

"They thought they were Bill's."

Maggie still didn't get it, and Mommie and I were too upset to stop and explain. We raced each other to the garage, and I backed the car out and we drove off without more explanations.

We pulled up at the Blue Place knowing we had missed Max; there was no car outside. We didn't stop. Without saying a word, I swung around the circle and headed for town.

At Ingram's office we entered, and I led the way to the inner office. There we found Max and Ingram with the brown paper spread out in front of them on the desk.

"Max!" Mommie burst out. "Those two women stole the paints!"

"No!"

"Yes!" I shouted.

"Well, do something! Don't just sit there!"

Both Ingram and Max were on their feet. Ingram said, "Good evening, ladies."

Max said, "Keep your shirts on."

The phone rang, and Ingram said, "Hello. . . . Yes, speaking. . . . Gone? . . . Sorry, boys, I called you as soon as I got the word—check with his sister again—you have? That's your best—— Thanks anyway. So long."

Max said, "Gone, eh?"

"Yep. They got there and they could see that he had occupied the place for the night, used the big office where the divan is—slept there. Found remains of some hamburgers and milk. But he was gone."

"He'll turn up." Max turned to Mommie and me.

"Well, girls, I'm sorry you went to all this trouble. The paints aren't too important."

"But you said——" I sputtered.

"I know, I know; I misled you. I sorted out Bill's paints long long ago. I wouldn't leave them around for anyone to pick up like that! You certainly underestimate my mentality—and I'm not the least bit flattered."

Mommie and I slumped to the nearest chairs. I won-

dered what was going to happen to me because I hadn't
yet told Max about Frankie.

Mommie said in a small, meek voice, "You have the
paints?"

Max nodded.

"And you know why——"

"No, we don't. But we'll figure it out presently."

I said, "What has the wrapping paper told you?"

Max and Ingram leaned over it once more. Mommie and
I peered over their shoulders.

Max traced the address with a spatulate finger. He read
aloud, "Mr. Edgar Pearson, care of the Keller Jewelry
Company, such and such a street, so and so. Now!

"Mr. Edgar Pearson is that old man I told you about
who came to claim the package more than a year ago. He
lacked the duty and left, presumably to raise the sum
somehow, get it out of an old sock or hold someone up for
it.

"He's old, like I said. He totters down the steps of the
Federal Building, still reading the card, probably mum-
bling to himself, and walks right behind a car that's backing
out of the parking lot next door. Zingo—he's dead.

"A crowd gathers, as crowds have a way of doing, and
the poor old guy is taken away in the basket and is sched-
uled for potter's field; he has no family and no money.
He's been a janitor for Keller Jewelry—well, not a janitor
exactly—more like a third-class handy man. The Keller
brothers step in and give the old duck a decent burial."

Mommie said, "And the man who backed into him?
Wasn't he insured?"

Max patted her copper-colored head. "Bright girl! No,
he—I mean—yes, he was insured, but he didn't do the
backing out. Someone was evidently about to steal the

car. The owner was up in the sixth floor of the building opposite, getting a haircut. Good thing he could prove it —this leaving the scene of the accident goes hard with ——"

I said, "Do you mean to tell me that a man could step into a stranger's car, back it out of the parking station, become involved in a major accident, and get out of the car and not have anyone see him?"

Ingram said, "Easiest thing in the world! What time of day, Johnson?"

"I was just getting back from lunch," said Max.

Ingram banged a fist into a palm. It sounded like a shot. "See what I mean? Everyone is on the street. How long does it take for a crowd to gather in the city at noon? About a second and a half!"

"But," I argued, "it doesn't take a second and a half to see someone get out of a car! Someone should have come forward with a description."

Max said, "The fact remains, no one did! And shut up! You're slowing my story. Where was I? Oh yes, the package.

"So the package was opened for inspection. We send out regular cards to the sender—it comes back in due time marked 'no one of this name at this address.' That kind of thing is happening all the time at Customs— that's why we have these auctions.

"Well, it doesn't take a mastermind to figure out that the sender's name is fictitious. The sender is a soldier, without a doubt, and he expected to get back here to the city, go to Pearson, and claim his package.

"Pearson's dead and gone. What does he do? He—the sender—shoots down to the Customs and gets in on the auction—but too late. Tracing the paints isn't too hard, and you know the rest."

"Why?" Mommie wailed.

I sat in silence and thought of Frankie. How could he have—he had said he was framed! If I told Ingram and Max, they would get him so fast he wouldn't have a chance to explain anything. If I could talk Max over to my way of thinking, perhaps he would be able to figure a way out.

Mommie was talking. "Why? What is so valuable—I can't see—that a man would kill——"

"Don't know yet," said Ingram, "but we'll figure it out in time, no doubt. The thing to do now is to locate Sorbus."

No! I couldn't! I wouldn't! The lad had called me, trusting me, and I had to take the chance that I was right and Ingram wrong. I stood up. It would be dark soon.

Mommie stood also. That brought Ingram and Max to their feet. Ingram said, "So long, Johnson, and thank you for this bit of corroboration."

Mommie said, "I don't see—the story is interesting, but what is he corroborating?"

"Oh," Max said, "I forgot to tell you. If you'd quit interrupting—— See this stamp? The commanding officer has to censor anything sent from overseas. Well, look closely."

Mommie and I got our heads together over the brown and wrinkled paper. It smelled a bit of old plaster. I couldn't make out the name. Mommie said, "I can see Captain—looks like Eagan—no——"

Ingram said, "It's E. A. Glenn."

I said, "Ernie Glenn! The one who——"

Max nodded. "The one who."

That made it nice!

Ingram walked to the door with us, shook hands with Max, who had to shift that awful umbrella from his right hand to his left. He said a pleasant good-by to Mommie and me.

I said, out on the sidewalk before my car, "What's he going to do?"

Max said, "Wait for the city police to pick Sorbus up!"

Mommie said, "I hope Grampie fed the children. What time is it getting to be?"

Max looked at his watch. "Almost eight o'clock. See you at the cove, Abbie."

I hesitated for a fraction of a second. Max had his hand on Mommie's elbow and was about to turn her toward his car. I said, "I'm not going home."

They turned puzzled faces. I opened the door of the car.

Max said, "What the hell——"

"I'm going——"

Max gave Mommie his keys and strode around my car, hooked that eternal umbrella over the back of the front seat and slipped under the wheel. He held out a hand for my keys. "I knew you were holding out on me, Abbie! You've looked like an inmate of that house on Ninety-second Street all afternoon."

Mommie leaned in at the window at my side of the car. "I take it that I'm to go on home and keep the fire up."

"You're a wonderful woman, Mommie."

"I think Abbie should tell me where you're going—in case I have to send out a posse."

I said, and my heart was in my mouth, "To the city line—to pick up Frankie Sorbus."

"Oh my God!" said Max. "Well, what are we waiting for?" He looked at his wife.

Mommie gave my arm a squeeze and left. Max started the car, did a U turn, and we started cityward. As soon as we had passed the outskirts he said, "Don't you think you had better tell me?"

I told him. When I finished I said, "I know you think I'm crazy——"

Max said, "Not necessarily. I've had an alternative that I could hardly credit, but——"

I said, "Alternative?"

"One of the Keller brothers."

"You're out of your mind!"

"No, I'm not! That package was sent to the janitor— the handy man."

"Max! They're rich men! They wouldn't be smuggling! They wouldn't be killing!"

"Just the same, Ingram and I have considered them. We can't find the reason yet—but——"

I said, "Have you questioned them—as to times and things like that?"

"Not yet! We——" Max slowed down and stopped at a red light. "Sorbus is more important right now."

Traffic was heavy, most of it coming from the city. We covered the rolling hilly road swiftly and much more smoothly than I could have driven; my old car doesn't drive so easily. As we neared the city I felt my heart quicken, the blood pound a little in my ears.

Max said, "Tell me again how we are to know him."

"He'll be on the lookout for me. You're to drive slowly around the first block in the city limits and he will appear from somewhere and hail me."

We reached the sign that announced the city. Max slowed to a crawl. It wasn't quite dark. I suggested that we pull up to the side of the street and wait for full dark. Max did.

We sat there for ten minutes, and nothing happened except that the darkness drew around us a little. I said, "Maybe we should go back to the outskirts and wait. He might be suspicious of a car that stands too long."

Max started up and drove out of the city again. We arrived once more at the sign and turned around very slowly. We turned the first corner to the right and cruised along the street. There were no lights, and it was pretty dark by then. And we seemed to be followed by another car very much like mine. I said so to Max.

He said, "Do you have any idea of how many Fords there were turned out in 'thirty-eight?" I kept still.

We rounded the corner and kept right again, still followed by the Ford. Max slowed down to a snail crawl. Nothing happened.

We rounded another corner, which brought us right back to the main road. The car behind us stopped. Max said, "This time, what do you say we turn left? He didn't specify which block, did he?"

I said, "No."

We crossed the main road; traffic had thickened considerably. We turned left. No one in sight. The other Ford crossed the main road and turned left. He followed our example and drove without lights. At the next corner we both turned left. That headed us right back toward the main road again.

I clutched Max by the arm. Ahead was a lone figure standing on the left side of the road.

Max quickened our pace slightly. The car behind us shot forward suddenly—I caught a glimpse of a kerchief-wrapped head—swerved left, and came to an abrupt stop at the man's side. The door on the driver's side opened; the driver slipped across the seat, leaving the wheel invitingly free.

Max made an exclamation of annoyance. He switched the headlights on; I recognized Frankie Sorbus as he slid into the seat and closed the door.

I cried out, "Frankie!"

He couldn't have heard me, for he let out the clutch, stepped on the gas, and shot around the corner into the traffic heading back toward the lake.

SEVENTEEN

Max swore. I had difficulty with my breathing. We got out into the stream of traffic once more, and I craned my neck to catch sight of the car. I finally located it three cars ahead.

I said, "He's three cars ahead."

Max was still swearing. He stopped long enough to say, "Don't let them out of your sight, and I'll work up there."

I said, "Who?"

Max said, "Looked like a woman."

"I wanted to say that but was afraid you'd laugh at me."

"What other woman would be interested in Sorbus?"

"She wasn't young—she was heavy—as heavy as I?"

"Right. What in the hell for——" Max swung left to go around the car ahead; someone on the other side of the road had the same idea; Max had to take his foot off the pedal and place it on the brake. We slewed to the side and slowed. A car got around us, and that made four between us and Frankie.

I said, "I can still see him. Do you suppose Frankie knew her?"

"I suppose Sorbus thought it was you."

"Where was he, Max?"

We passed the car immediately in front and the second.

There was a light, where another main highway crossed the one we were on. He shot across.

Max said, "He had a key to the store—Keller's. He holed up there. Orrin Keller called Ingram after he left us this afternoon. Probably from the hotel, when he let the two dames off. He was worried when he remembered the key."

The light changed. Max shot ahead of the two cars before us—they gave us definitely dirty looks—and we were off. Two miles and we came in sight of the taillight that should be Frankie. Max made a satisfied sound in his throat.

"Where in the world is he going?"

"You got me."

"Old Village or Ogg Lake—looks like to me."

The taillight disappeared in a dip in the road, and I knew that beyond that dip the road forked. To the right the West Lake Road; to the left the foot of the lake and the East Lake Road. I felt the car jump a little as Max pressed down with his foot. The headlights of the oncoming cars hit my eyes with the same steadying rhythm as the blood in my throat, my temples, my ears. I held my breath.

We swooped down into the dip, swooped out again, passed two cars on the brow, two cars that were not Fords. The fork lay a half-mile ahead. There was a pin point of red up there; it turned left.

I said, "Is that he?"

"I hope." It was a prayer. We swung left. I looked down the road to the right as we zoomed past. A million red taillights. My stomach flopped sickeningly. I didn't tell Max.

The next two miles, I knew, were winding and then straightened out for the last two before either turning right for the East Lake Road or keeping straight on for the last mile to Old Village. We covered the two miles without a glimpse of the car we wanted. We passed innumerable others; I craned my neck for each one, swiveled it back, and faced the zoom—zoom—zoom of the oncoming cars.

Max said, as we rounded the last turn and straightened, "He'll never go through Old Village."

"Where—where—where do you think he's going?"

"I haven't the faintest. Your house?"

I was silent. He had said—— Max made that satisfied sound again, and I peered forward. Yes! There was the taillight we wanted. Up until that moment I had never realized that a taillight could be individual. They can. This one was oval in shape, which didn't mean a thing until we could get up close enough to distinguish the ovalness. But once in a while I could see that it was oval. It had a little heart of blue. That also couldn't be made out until we were fairly close. It was placed on the left side of the car, and its mate on the right wasn't working or was non-existent. And the light that should have been on the license was blurred, at any rate. We hadn't yet gotten close enough to make it out.

It disappeared around a car. We passed the car and caught it again. We came to the fork in the road. It turned right. Max groaned.

I said, "What's the matter?"

"We'll lose him as sure as shooting. You know this Lake Road on a holiday!"

"By that same token, we may catch him," I argued. "You know the Lake Road on a holiday!"

"You watch the cars we pass, the ones standing. I'll watch the ones ahead."

We wove in and out of the curves on the narrow road,

slower now. Once in a while we caught our taillight again. We reached the turnoff to the cove and passed it. I clutched Max's arm. He shook me off.

"He is!" Max exclaimed.

"The Blue Place!" I said.

"Looks as though!" We swerved sharply left; the tiny red taillight was halfway up the haunted-house road. There were no other cars in sight, just the two of us chummily pell-melling up into the hills.

We turned right, on two wheels, and wove along the curves of the Hog Back, straightened out for the last stretch that was the Ridge. The sign that said "Dead End," which meant we were on the Marrowback, loomed in my mind minutes before we reached it. I felt icy. I could hear Max breathing heavily beside me. He swung the wheel around right again and we were on the last lap. He slowed a little; the ruts wouldn't permit the pace we had been hitting. He turned out the lights as we cleared the trees and came in sight of the circular driveway in front of the house.

The car was parked a small way beyond the porch. And the lights were on in the house, those ugly, bare bulbs glaring down from the ceilings. We could see the two easy chairs drawn up, one on either side of the low table, in front of the paint-smeared picture window. Max turned off the engine. We both got out of the car. Max came around to my side of the car, and we stood a moment looking up at the house. It was quiet. There was no sound. The car beside us made a small ticking noise as it cooled off, and as soon as that came through the beating of the pulse in my ears, I was conscious of the car ahead making the same regular crackle.

Frankie Sorbus stood in the doorway, a hand high on

either side of the screen. He said, "I thought I heard some-one come up behind us. Is that you, Miss Harris?"

"Well," I said, "we certainly had a time catching you! I thought you wanted me to pick you up!" I walked up the path, bending down and retrieving a bright-colored kerchief that lay there.

Frankie said, "I told you I'd meet you here! Was that you who followed us?"

"Max and I." I stepped up on the porch. Frankie held the screen open, and I went inside. Max followed.

A soft and slithery voice spoke from behind me. "Put up the hands."

"What!" I exclaimed.

Orrin spoke again, and I didn't even turn around. I was afraid. I never have been so afraid in my life. There was something in that voice, which carried to us and no farther, that froze me where I was. I am sure that had someone been standing on the other side of the screen in the open door, he would not have heard Orrin's voice.

He said, "Please do not move, either one of you. Sorbus will look you over for weapons. Do that, will you, please, Sorbus?"

Frankie went over Max, who had said nothing at all. Max was afraid too. That realization came over me with a companion piece of wonder. It had never occurred to me that Max could know fear.

The controlled voice behind me said, "Nothing? Good! Now the lady!"

Frankie looked up at the man with distaste, refusal in the motion of his hands, which flew to his sides.

The voice said, "Sorbus!" And its very softness was menacing. Frankie went over me gingerly. I tried to smile at him.

"Nothing? Good again! Now, you three, move slowly into the other room." The light in the old kitchen clicked off. He must have reached behind him; the switch was very near the entrance.

"Very slowly, please. The lady first, then Sorbus, and then Johnson. Wait!"

We stopped and stood like statues, not looking back, but all three facing the open, lighted doorway. We waited.

The voice said, "When you get there, the lady will sit in the large chair facing us, Johnson will sit in the one opposite, and Sorbus will lie down on the floor under the window. We're going to have a nice talk!"

We stood perfectly still, saying nothing.

"What's the matter? Get going!" The voice harshened a little. We moved slowly to the lighted room. I sat down gingerly on the edge of the big chair and found myself facing him.

"Settle back in the chair; you aren't going anywhere," said Orrin. I forced myself to see him. He stood in the doorway, a gun leveled in our direction. A very businesslike number that I thought I remembered seeing before. Then I realized that those particular army Colts were a dime a dozen right now. Most of the boys just out of the Army had one. I sat back in the chair, but I had trouble leaning against the back. My own spine didn't want to bend.

Max was having no trouble that way. He was slouched down in the deep seat as if he were settling down to the evening paper. Frankie sat on the floor under the window.

Orrin said, "I told you to lie down."

Frankie lay down—on his side, with his head on his arms and facing us. The cartons of junk were still there. He pressed up against them, tight.

Orrin said, "You may turn your back, Sorbus. This talk

I'm going to have with Miss Harris and Mr. Johnson does not concern you. I won't need you until I'm ready for you to suicide."

Frankie swallowed and turned over. His body knocked against the cartons at the knees and where his wrists touched them.

Max looked around his chair and up at Orrin, looked as quickly away.

Orrin said, "Now! Let's get down to business. Where are they?"

"I might ask you that," said Max.

Orrin said, "Now listen to me! I'll state what I have to tell you once and only once." His voice hadn't risen a jot, yet it suggested a menace that could be measured; that is, measured in relationship to that which had gone before. It had developed.

"Are you ready?" Orrin still faced me. He could neither see nor be seen by Max. I looked up quickly, and away as quickly as Max had done. I wouldn't have known Orrin: white as asparagus is white when it has been covered for its entire growing period, a green cast, waxy. And the eyes sunken, quite mad!

Max made a quick backward gesture with his hand.

Orrin jerked. His voice lost a little of its control. "One more move like that, my man, and I'll find the stuff all by myself."

Max became still. He was breathing through his mouth, as was I. Breath through the nostrils seemed to make a whistling sound. His eyes met mine, and the conviction that not one of the three of us was going to get out of this place was a fetid, fusty, miasmal reality. It stank in our nostrils; it tasted foul in our open mouths; we were absorbing the poison of it through the pores of our skin.

The dread silence continued. "You're going to tell me where those paints disappeared to this afternoon. Then this—this toothache on the floor is going to sign a confession and take his own life, the coward, and you can go home."

But we knew he lied. We'd never go home!

There was silence in the old house. There were no night noises up here on the top of the world. Away off in the woods I could hear a whippoorwill, but faintly, like a ghostly memory of all the country nights in my life. There wasn't even a clock in the house.

Orrin cleared his throat. I felt I had to speak.

I said, "The two—those two—Iris Rutland and her friend Gladys—they—they fooled around a lot in Max's boat—perhaps they took them?"

Now what made me say that? My very tone was false; it wasn't going to fool anyone. Max's lips formed a "Bravo!" I brightened. Did he want me to do the talking?

Orrin said, "I was there! They didn't take anything but their own silly stuff. I took the paints. Only I took the wrong ones. Someone was there before me."

No one spoke. I saw Max's eyes roll a little. It frightened me more than Orrin's suppressed, compelling tones had. Max said, "Make me believe we'll get out of here alive."

"I'm under no obligation to make you any promises. I say you'll get out of here because I wish it—for no other reason."

"Make me believe it!"

"Johnson, I tell you, get going on where they are. I'm going to know."

"What's in the paints?"

"You know!"

"I can guess, knowing your business, but I don't know."

"Well, you're right. Now produce them."

"I don't have them on me."

"Where are they?"

"Out in the car."

"Exactly?"

"On the back seat."

Orrin sighed. I couldn't look at him. I think I closed my eyes. I could sense his relish nevertheless.

Max said, "Shall I go for them?"

Orrin laughed. A happy and benevolent laugh. "Don't bother, my lad. You sit right here and relax. I'll step out of the door and pick up the pretty things myself. And I'll keep this"—he brandished the gun—"right on the door. There's only one—door, I mean. I'll be back in a minute, and we can finish this little talk. And you wouldn't be fooling me, would you?"

"I wouldn't be fooling you. On the back seat."

Orrin backed out of the door slowly. I didn't move. Max sat perfectly still. I felt Frankie twitch on the floor at my feet. My eyes opened and fastened on the open doorway.

The muzzle of the gun appeared once more. All the blood in my body dropped somewhere, as the bath water does when you pull the plug. Orrin's voice said, "I'm not going to go out to the car for a few minutes. I would like you, Miss Harris, to close your eyes so that you do not see me when I do leave. And I'll be back, almost instantly. I wouldn't want you to do anything foolish, like getting up out of those chairs."

We gave no answer. I closed my eyes, pinched them down into my head.

There was a whisper of sound from the other room. A rustling that might have been the door opening and closing, might have been the barest ghost of a man moving about, and then utter silence. I stopped breathing. I opened my eyes and they met Max's. I made a gesture as if to get up. He shook his head in the negative, and obediently I sank deeper into my chair.

There was a shot from outside. The house fell apart, the sky shattered, the hill beneath us disintegrated entirely, and I sat attached to the chair with my eyes closed.

Max was shaking me. The room was full of men, men in blue uniforms and leather straps across their chests and around their waists and guns in their hands.

I never saw Orrin Keller again.

EIGHTEEN

Max and I arrived back at the cove well after eleven. Max ran the car into the garage and we walked around the house. No one on our porch. Mommie called from the group of chairs out under the cottonwoods in front of the Johnsons' cottage. We went over.

Grampie and Maggie shared the long seat. Mommie and Virginia each occupied a chair pulled up on either side at an angle. Virginia jumped up, offering me her chair, but I chose to snuggle down between my sister and Grampie. It was wonderful! I reached out and took a hand on either side of me and hung on.

Max dropped to the ground beside his wife and said, "Rub my back and I'll tell you."

Mommie said, "You better!" and started a rhythmic figure-eight motion with her hand between Max's shoulders, which she was to keep up the whole time we were there—a considerable while.

Virginia said, "Bill's coming home tomorrow!" Bells

were ringing in her voice. "He never felt better in his life! We're going to sail; he's going to teach me to ride a surfboard; he learned in the islands. And . . ." Her voice trailed off dreamily. There were no doubts, no hesitations in Virginia's manner. All that panic of yesterday afternoon was missing. I suppose Virginia had had a good look at her own family tree and found the horse thief hanging there. We each have one, at least. And Bill's cousin, the other Bill, had paid for his sin; paid with his life.

"Will called," said Maggie, "around ten."

"What did you tell him?" I asked.

"Everything! I feel he has a right to know. We talked for over forty-five minutes; he'll have some hotel bill this week! He still feels that Bill will be all right with us, especially as he seems to be happy. And Will is going to try and pay us a visit late in August when he can get away."

"Good," I said.

Max said, "Ingram tells me I have you to thank, Mommie, for the marines."

"Did I do wrong?"

"You did exactly right! How did you know enough——"

Mommie's hand didn't stop moving; it hardly paused, but there was a change in the rhythm. She smiled. She said, "I got that look you tossed toward Ingram's office— I had a feeling that you and Abbie were walking into something, and I wanted Ingram to back you. Was I right?"

"You were absolutely right!"

"Ingram said I was. He said he didn't mind sending a few boys out just in case, and he said he didn't mind your not telling him everything as long as it worked out right. But if it didn't, look out! He'd raise merry ned!"

Max snorted. Mommie continued.

"So he sent three cars out on the main road, one to stop at the town line, one to stop at the fork in the road at the foot of the lake, and one to follow you to the end, and all three to follow you if you headed back this way. Which they did, didn't they?"

I said, "I didn't see them."

Max said, "Neither did I. But then we weren't looking for them. I suppose they used their two-ways to keep Ingram informed, and I suppose he gave them orders not to let us—not to annoy us—to give us our heads and step in only if things broke against us. That's why they must have walked the last quarter mile when we were holed in at the Blue Place."

I shuddered. Mommie and Grampie came forward in their chairs. Maggie squeezed my hand.

"Well, don't stop!" cried Virginia. "Tell us about that!"

Max outlined the ride and the scene in the Blue Place for them. He made it sound very tame; I could feel the same smothered sensations I had felt at the time.

I said, "Did you have any idea Ingram would get there?"

Max said, "I saw him through the window, and I was petrified Keller would too—that's why I made Keller go out to the car."

"And that," I said, "is why you wouldn't let me get up when Orrin left?"

"Right! What could you have done?"

"I'd have done something." I said, "Were they—the paints—really in the car?"

"In the old umbrella!"

"Suppose Ingram hadn't surrounded the house?"

Max shrugged. "I'd have stalled a little longer, hoping I could think of something. I'd have given him the paints—

what do I care about a million dollars when he had the gun! And he couldn't have gotten away with it unless he killed us all——"

That speech took a little explaining. Some of the group didn't know about the paints. Max explained that he really had stumbled onto the idea of the paints that afternoon, as he had already told Mommie and me.

"Actually," he said, "there is so little smuggling in our small Customs—it's been years since anyone has tried it— we couldn't be blamed for letting it pass. We should know that—— No, we shouldn't! Paints are a legitimate import. My gosh, the stuff some of those boys have sent back! And Keller showed no interest the day of the auction. He was all worked up because he had taken time to come down to look at the Italian costume jewelry stuff that wasn't worth the duty! How were we to know he was all worked up because he didn't get the paints?"

Grampie said, "I take it the smuggling concerned jewels? That would be what Keller would be interested in."

"What else?" said Max. "Ingram opened a couple of tubes and then just locked the whole thing up in his safe. He was scared to handle the stuff. I was too sick of the sight of it to care, but by tomorrow I suppose I'll be champing at the bit! Especially as they now belong to me!"

Mommie took her hand away and screamed softly, "Max! And you expect me to sit here rubbing your back!"

"Get back on the job, wench, or I'll stop talking."

Mommie hugged herself. "I thought it was just a figure of speech when you told me to stick with you and I'd wear diamonds!" She resumed her rubbing.

Max said, "There's a little matter of Bill—I'll get together with him tomorrow."

Mommie said, "Of course! I forgot Bill! They all belong

to him." She tried, unsuccessfully, not to sound disappointed.

I said, "Don't be silly! Bill gave them to you, and besides that, where would he be——"

Max said, "You women keep out of this. Bill and I will take care of it."

Grampie said, "Who sent them? Begin at the beginning and go slowly."

"'Unidentifiable' is the way the name of the sender is entered in the books. We all know it was Sorbus, but I'll bet the value of the stones against a plugged nickel that no one could make him admit it! He was so surprised when Ingram didn't throw him into jail. Keller kept screaming how he did it all for the lad!

"And another thing, I'm going to be surprised if Keller isn't in need of a fairish sum of money. Even a million dollars isn't motive enough to kill, unless there was the additional pressure of necessity."

Maggie said, in her soft voice, "Where did these mythical jewels come from?"

"Germany, of course," said Max. "Easy enough to open the bottom of a lead-foil tube, tuck in a stone, seal it again. Take up no space at all. And you can hold a million dollars' worth of jewels in the palm of one hand."

Grampie growled, "I said, 'Begin at the beginning and go slowly.' This way you're only confusing us."

There was a pause; we waited. I saw Mommie raise a hand and examine her palm. Max began finally: "Frank Sorbus—we better begin with him—has worked for the brothers Keller since he was a kid. The last few years he's been Orrin's henchman, exclusively.

"Now! Let's take Frank's character. A good egg—not too bright—not too honest—not too brave, either. He would never, in this world, do a thing like murder—nothing could matter that much to Sorbus—he isn't capable of caring enough about anything, even a million dollars, to kill. Easy come, easy go—that would be him.

"Now we'll go to Germany with Sorbus: he was with the first occupational troops. Without a doubt he and his pals picked up a safe and pried it open with some army dynamite. Naturally he'd turn to Keller—jewels—right up his alley. The paint idea wouldn't be difficult for Keller to dream up. Sorbus, I'm sure, wasn't capable of contriving that stunt himself, but he'd be able to follow instructions, fix it up, consign it to the janitor.

"A year goes by.

"Sorbus is let out of the Army.

"Keller misses the package of jewel-filled paint tubes by a matter of minutes. Does he give up and write it off to profit and loss, as Sorbus would? He does not. He gets busy the very next day—I'm wrong—that very night—he starts haunting Abbie because he knows it is her nephew who bought the paints. And he sticks to her, through two murders and one attempt, until he finds them.

"Now! Let us switch to the Captain Glenn. He was the commanding officer who passed the package. Without a doubt he knew what was going on all around him over there, and all he had to do was to select the GI with the largest take and close in on him after they both got back to this country. He happened to select Sorbus as a likely prospect for blackmail.

"Knuckle-headed Sorbus doesn't suspect a man like Keller of murder. So when Glenn puts the pressure on Sorbus, he in turn runs to Keller, who takes over the handling of Glenn." Max nodded in my direction. I nodded back. I knew when! I had heard Glenn putting on the pressure! Max went on.

"Sorbus takes his girl home. Keller pretends to get chummy with Glenn; gets him to do the driving when they go after the paints, which they think are in the back of Bill's car."

I shivered. Mommie said, "Why didn't Sorbus send the paints to his sister? Let her hold them till he got back? Why Keller?"

Max sounded impatient. "And where else would he send them but to someone who could sell them? We'll never know how much Keller has disposed of in that line already. Poor old Pearson trotted up to that Customs more than once."

I said, "But why did he run over him? Or was that an honest-to-goodness accident?"

"I don't know. Probably never will. Keller may have thought he was suspected at Customs—may have thought poor Pearson was getting suspicious—he certainly knew about the auction rule; he's been to many. And it may have been a real accident. That would account for his panic—a whole year of knowing that there was a million dollars lying around the corner from him, waiting, perhaps needing it, and then worrying for fear someone would get in ahead of him!"

Grampie said, "I haven't straightened out those guns yet."

"I told you," said Max, "one gun belonged to Rutland. I suppose that night Keller set out to search the Blue Place, or perhaps he intended to dicker with the boy—he didn't know at that time that there were two—found the place open, and obeyed the impulse to look around. I maintain the guy was impulsive, an opportunist.

"He must have been surprised by a returning Rutland. The gun lay in the top tray of the trunk. He shot Rutland.

"A forty-five holds eight shots, with one in the chamber, nine. Keller hung onto the gun, used it again on Glenn, and then planted it in Sorbus' car along with the wallet of money.

"Sorbus says that he, Keller, was waiting up for him when he got home last night. Keller gave Sorbus a line about the police looking for him, built a nice circumstantial story against Sorbus, and frightened him so that he did exactly as Keller wished—he hid. Keller suggested the store; it was closed over the long week end."

I said, "Then Sorbus had nothing to do with the murders—didn't know——"

"Nope," said Max. "A little slow, our Sorbus. Alone in the city, hiding in the holiday-closed store, he figured things out finally—the hard way, no doubt. He calls Abbie.

"Keller, busy pumping Abbie, hears the phone call. It didn't take a mastermind to guess the source, to realize the significance of the words 'City line.' All he has to do is beat Abbie to the rendezvous—a cinch. And I'll bet he didn't even hold a gun on Sorbus on that last ride!"

I said to my sister, "Bill's gun is gone."

"I know. I took it."

Grampie said, "How did Keller get Frank's car?"

"Easy," said Max. "After he left us, late this afternoon, he had his brother George run him in as far as the city line, caught a bus to the police station, claimed the car, which was really his, and then hung around the city line waiting for Sorbus and you, Abbie. I think he knew I'd string along. He was smart enough to tie his daughter's scarf around his head to imitate friend Abbie."

Once more Maggie squeezed my hand. She cleared her

throat. "Did those drunken hussies—did they—— Orrin
Keller couldn't know they would create a diversion so he
could swipe the paints out of the boat, did he?"

Max made a derisive sound. "Lord no! Just additional
proof to my contention that Keller was an opportunist. He
came that afternoon—this afternoon—indulging himself
in his favorite sport—pumping Abbie. You see, he had lost
track of the paints once more."

"In a rut, wasn't he?" interrupted Mommie.

"Obviously Abbie told him the paints were in my boat,
or he wouldn't have made the grab for them."

I sighed again. I was hungry. I realized suddenly that
I had had no dinner. I said, "I'm hungry."

Max said, "And I bet you forgot to buy some beer,
Mommie."

She said, "Oh no, I didn't! I mean, oh yes, I did."

We broke up the group quite naturally. Max and
Mommie to their own kitchen and the cold beer, Maggie
and I to ours and a Welsh rabbit, Virginia to her sleeping
porch and dreams of Bill, no doubt.

Grampie said, "I guess I'll sit out here awhile. I like
to watch the lights go out across the lake."